I0640395

BUGGED

"Next time you want to take in a speakeasy, don't go to one of those lower caste ones. They exist on all levels, my boy; Effective, Engineer, and Technician. When the urge hits you, let me know."

The eyes of the younger man widened. "You mean, you belong to one yourself?"

William Morris chuckled. "No microphones, no bugs, Rex. Certainly you must realize that one of the privileges of my rank, even though I'm retired, is that there is no monitoring of my home. You're as free here as in a speakeasy, and considerably safer."

THE COSMIC EYE

Mack Reynolds

WILDSIDE PRESS

Copyright © MCMLXIX by Mack Reynolds

THE COSMIC EYE

by Mack Reynolds

*When four sit down to conspire, three
are police spies and the other a fool.*
—Old European Proverb

1.

"My dear boy," William Morris said, bending his
chubby knees to adjust to the acceleration of the elevator,
"I am sure I have no need to warn you, ah . . . well, to
not express any of your father's less popular opinions this
afternoon." He cleared his throat apologetically. "That is,
of course . . ." He let the sentence dribble away.

Rex laughed reassuringly. "Great Scott, Uncle Bill,
stop worrying about me. Taos isn't as wild and wooly as
you seem to think. We're really quite civilized out there.
And Dad doesn't exactly go about making anti-Technate
speeches from soapboxes, for that matter."

"Well," his uncle said. "I should hope not." The older
man cast his eyes quickly about the elevator compartment. "I do wish you wouldn't say things like that, my
boy."

"Say what? All that I said was that Dad didn't make a
practice of saying things against the government."

His uncle was worried. "Yes, but flippantly. It's easy
enough to get into a habit of speaking flippantly, quickly
and . . . well, before you know it you've actually allowed

your subconscious . . . to, well." He stopped and cleared his throat. He was a roly-poly man in his sixties his hair gone completely gray but obviously in the top of vigorous, energetic health.

Rex Morris, his nephew, was pushing thirty, pushing five feet ten, pushing one sixty. But he looked as though thus far life itself hadn't pushed him very hard. He wore an easy going, all but indolent air, the rich young aristocrat to a T. He grinned at the older man now.

Uncle Bill was unhappy with him. "You know what I mean," he said severely. "Here we are. Lizzy Mihm's penthouse. Having an apartment like this gives you some idea of her prestige, my boy."

"Who is she again? I've met so many people these last few days, that I lose track.

"Well, you ought to remember Elizabeth Mihm. You met her the other night at Technician Philp's party at the Elite Room. Her husband used to be Prime Technician of the Transport Functional Sequence. Good friend of mine. Since he passed on, Lizzy has devoted a good deal of her time to entertaining. Her apartment is quite a center, quite a place for you to make contacts, my boy. She has the Supreme Technician himself to her soirees, quite often."

They left the elevator, emerged into an ultra-swank entrada, and stood before a door. The older man pushed a button at its side and smiled knowledgeably at his nephew. "Swank, eh? An electric button. Lizzy Mihm is famous for her antiques."

Rex Morris was intrigued. "What does it do?"

"It rings a bell inside. Then Lizzy knows someone is at the door and responds."

Rex looked at his uncle blannly. "Then what?"

"Then she comes to the door to see who it is."

"But look, why not just have an identity screen on the door like everyone else? Then she can see who it is and decide whether or not she wants to open up at all."

His uncle said impatiently, "It's an antique, don't you understand? I don't imagine a half dozen people in the whole city have them."

6

Rex Morris muttered something to that, but the door was opening.

"Why, *William*," Lizzy Mihm gushed. "And your *dear*, sweet nephew from the wild, *wild* West."

Rex Morris winced.

"*Do* come in," she fluttered, sweeping a hefty and heavily bejeweled arm in the direction of the sounds of her party. She was a middle aged biddy, not more than five foot two and going to lard by the minute. However, she had a pleasant enough face, in the German hausfrau tradition. It came to Rex Morris that aristocrats in person seldom resembled in person the glamorous projections you saw on the Tri-Di shows.

"Of course you remember Rex," William Morris said, giving his hostess a peck on the cheek in the way of greeting.

"Why, of *course*, and there are some dear, dear people I want him to meet this afternoon. Including," she added archly, "a dear, *dear* young lady." She laid a beefy hand on Rex Morris' arm as they filed into the inner rooms.

"William," she said over her shoulder, "you know your way around. You can take care of yourself."

Uncle Bill headed for the nearest autobar.

She said, "Now Rex. I may call you Rex, of course . . ."

"Of course, Techna Mihm."

She giggled. "Actually, everyone calls me Elizabeth, so you may, too. But just a word before I take you around. Now everybody, *everybody* has a wonderful time at my affairs. Oh, *wonderful*. Just remember, of course, that we don't discuss religion or politics, or anything else controversial, and, of course, nothing has ever been said in my home against the government."

"Why, certainly not," Rex said.

She patted his arm. "Ummm," she said approvingly. "I remember your father when he was a young man. I see you have retained only his better qualities."

There didn't seem to be any answer to that. Lizzy Mihm swept him up to a group of ladies who were currently listening to the complaints of a breathless member of their gathering, obviously expressing strong opinions on a matter of the greatest importance.

"Butter," she was saying indignantly. "My dears, I simply don't know what to do about the servant problem. Real whale butter, mind you, for greasing herself and there's no breaking her of it. She's one of the old family robos, one of the very early models that I've had all my life and my mother before me. So what can you do? You can't just have her reconditioned, what would everyone say? But she uses *butter*. Heavens knows how my grandparents could have afforded it. I know I can't. Butter, my dears, three thousand erg units a pound. What I mean is . . ."

"Servants!" one of the other ladies said, casting her eyes ceilingward.

Somewhere along the route of introductions, Rex Morris acquired a drink. He met this individual, that individual, was introduced sweepingly to this whole group, that whole group. Had a few meaningless words said to him by this one, said a few meaningless words to that one. He retained possibly one name out of ten.

Lizzy Mihn finally stopped to reorganize. She took up a glass of wine from one of the autobars and sipped it. "Too cold," she said, frowning. "Servants!" She added absently, as her eyes darted about her apartment, hostess-like. "I wonder if things were better before, when there were human servants."

Rex lifted his eyebrows. "My dear Techna Mihn."

Her eyes shot to his face, widened. "Oh, don't misunderstand. I wasn't criticising the government. The Service Functional Sequence was antiquated and due for discontinuation."

"I don't know anything about it," Rex Morris said primly.

"Of course not, neither do I."

"Who is that very attractive woman over there?" Rex said, obviously changing the subject. They were dangerously close to the controversial. "The one talking to the big Security official."

"Over there with Technician Matt Edgeworth? Oh, Na-

8

dine," Lizzy Mihm said. "Didn't I introduce you to Techna Nadine Sims?"

"I don't think so," Rex said. "I certainly would have remembered. She's certainly the most stunning young woman present. Is she the dear, dear young lady you mentioned?"

"Well, no," Lizzy Mihm said. There was an uncomfortable element in her voice. "To tell you the *truth,* I understand Nadine is, well, said to be connected with the SFS."

"Oh," Rex said. "How nice."

Lizzy Mihm said hurriedly, "Now, Rex, you know your uncle is an old, *old* friend of mine and, of course, I knew your father too, before he huffed out there to wherever it is he . . ."

"Taos," Rex said, still eyeing the girl across the room. She was a slender, quiet sophisticated product, clad simply in a gray sari. There seemed to be a certain feline aura about her, a black panther in the jungle, incredibly beautiful but obviously dangerous. The big police official had gone off somewhere now. Rex wondered whether it was her connection with the Security SF that accounted for the absence of the admirers that should have been banked three or four deep in her vicinity.

"Yes, of course," his hostess was saying. "What I mean is, Rex, I have your interests very, very deeply at heart. William tells me that you've finished your studies and are seeking an appointment in a suitable functional sequence. And, well, we do want you to make the *right* contacts."

Rex looked down at her, amused. "You mean Techna Sims isn't to be considered a good contact?"

She tapped his arm with a hefty hand. "Now, you stop Rex Morris. I know you're joshing me. Isn't that a wonderful word? Joshing. Absolutely antique. It means you were jesting with me. I was only reminding you that you're a newcomer to the capital and it's even more necessary than usual not to be, well, considered interested in controversial matters. And Nadine *might* be . . . well, you know. But do come along, I can see you're intrigued now."

9

Nadine Sims gave him an overly ready smile. "I was wondering when we'd be introduced," she said. "Our celebrities come few and far between these days."

"Celebrities?" Rex Morris said.

"The son of Leonard Morris makes interesting meeting," she told him, her eyes going up and down his trim, expensively suited figure and obviously liking what they saw.

Lizzy Mihm fluttered, "Now I'll just leave you young people and check on things. I do believe I heard the doorbell." She bustled off.

"Quite an old girl," Rex said, looking for something to say.

"The capital's most successful hostess," Nadine said. "All the very best people never miss a Mihm party. I hear that you are in town for good."

He grinned at her. "That sounds like a terrible thing to say about any thirty year old bachelor."

She frowned slightly, quizzically, and on her it looked fine. She said, "I beg your pardon?"

He did a mock leer. "Far from being in town for good, I'm wide open to any suggestions about what the capital offers in the way of bad. You see the evil reputation of Greater Washington has spread, yea even to the wilds— and it sounds wonderful."

She laughed at him. "I'll have to offer my guide services. What I meant was, you're in town permanently."

"Only if I can find an appointment that seems promising. Uncle Bill is optimistic, however." He yawned slightly, as though at the prospect of going to work.

"I think I'd enjoy another Susskratzer," she said, strolling toward the nearest autobar, as they talked. "Is your specialty the same as your father's?"

He dialed her a glass of the sparkling wine and grimaced. "That's the difficulty. I'm incurably lazy. I haven't specialized in anything." He handed her the chilled glass.

She raised her eyebrows over the rim of the glass even as she sipped. "You shock me. What is the Technician class coming to?"

Rex Morris shrugged and dialed himself a Sazerac.

10

"Too much trouble. And, besides, all it gets you is difficulty. Look at my dad, the scientist who conquered the virus diseases. But is that what he is primarily known for? Of course not. His fame is based on his refusal to conform and . . ."

"Techno Morris," she said gently. "I don't believe we really know each other this well do we?"

He was immediately repentive. "Sorry."

She gave him her ready smile. "I know what you mean. And I see your position. And with your connections, what need is there to specialize? You couldn't fail to wind up on top if you tried."

Before they could develop that further, the hulking Security Technician, Matt Edgeworth, with whom she'd been talking earlier, came up and after a somewhat stiff and overly formal invitation, swept Nadine Sims away toward a room that had been cleared for dancing. She looked back over her shoulder at Rex and grimaced hopelessly, as though she would rather have remained.

Rex Morris pursed his lips in a silent appreciative whistle as he looked after her. The sari dress of the Indian women is one of the most flattering feminine garments ever designed and the figure of Nadine Sims was already such that it needed very little flattery indeed.

A voice at his elbow said in a drawn out, "V-e-r-y bad, my dear boy."

Rex turned to his uncle, "What?"

"Nothing. Nothing at all, Rex. How are you enjoying yourself?"

"Fine. Lot of nice people, Uncle Bill."

"How do you like, ah, Techna Sims?"

"Pretty girl, all right. Beautiful would be the better word."

"That she is. Ah, well . . . I understand she sometimes does chores for . . ." he hesitated.

"For the Security FS," Rex finished for him. "So they tell me."

His uncle cleared his throat. "Want you to meet some other friends of mine, my dear boy. Technician Marrison over here is a mucky-muck in the Textile F.S. Always

11

looking for new blood, you know, especially with the early retirement ages we have now."

Technician Marrison, a chubby, balding, red nosed executive type, was in the midst of what he evidently considered to be a hilarious affair when Rex and his uncle came up.

". . . and then we switched to Hawaiians," he related. "Four parts gin, two of orange juice, one curacao. Served in a hollowed out pineapple, you know. By this time we were all kinked. Absolutely kinked. You should've seen Jeff. Jeff was kinked. And Martha . . ."

"Martha?" someone interrupted. "Not Martha. Martha has a capacity like a camel. I've never seen Martha . . ."

"Kinked," Technician Marrison insisted happily. "And then we all took off for the Flop House, carrying these pineapples, understand. Really hilarious. Each of us had a pineapple in each hand."

"Is that where the SFS effective stopped you?" somebody else laughed.

"Did we tell *him* where to head in," Marrison chuckled. "Imagine, there we were, two Prime Technicians and three Technicians and this numbskull tries to pull *his* authority on us."

Everyone laughed.

Uncle Bill interrupted to say, "Fred, I wanted to introduce you to my nephew. This is Rex. Rex, Fredrick Marrison is Technician of the Textile Functional Sequence for the whole eastern seaboard."

Marrison visibly puffed. He shook hands condescendingly. "Your nephew?" he said to William Morris. And then, less jovially, "Not the son of your brother, Leonard?"

Rex Morris nodded. "Leonard Morris is my father."

Marrison made a face. "Well, I admire your father's researches into the viruses, of course, everybody does, however, I could never appreciate his . . ."

Lizzy Mihm had swept up. "Gentlemen, gentlemen," she twittered, "we're not arguing anything over here, are we? Rex, you come along with me. I want you to meet a dear, *dear* friend of mine."

12

In view of the fact that his uncle could probably speak his case more effectively than he, Rex Morris allowed himself to be led off, after some routine banality to the textile potentate.

In fact, his head was still turned back to the last group, when Lizzy Mihm said, "Paula Klein, here is the dear boy I mentioned I was going to introduce you to. The nice, *nice* boy. Rex Morris from, how do you say it, Touse?"

"Taos," Rex said. "Rhymes with house, or mouse, or . . . well, hello."

Paula Klein frowned at him. He got the vague feeling that in this pretty girl's life meeting someone in her own age bracket could be considered a waste of time better devoted to more important matters. She must have been in her mid-twenties, he decided, but she had the serious, sincere air of the sophomore on ideals bent. A shame, he had decided already, since her brunette looks were exactly of the type he liked best. Hair so black as to be suspect, dark eyes, a creamy complexion almost as dark as the Indians of his native Taos. Her mouth was naturally red and generous, and her teeth were the most perfect he could remember having seen.

". . . her mother," Lizzy Mihm was saying, "one of my *dearest* friends." She patted Rex on the arm with one beefy paw, Paula with the other. "Now you two get to know each other." She added, archly, "But mind yourselves. I'm afraid Rex's father has an unfortunate reputation for discussing politics, and, of course, Paula's grandfather and his religion . . ." She giggled to indicate how bold she was being and swept off.

Rex Morris pulled his thinking away from Paula's physical attributes, excellent as they might be, and said, "Grandfather's religion?"

Paula Klein said expressionlessly, "I believe Lizzy rather insists on no politics or religion, no sex, no criticism of current institutions, no race of other controversial subjects, and *above all* . . ."

Rex chimed in with her and together they chanted, *"No criticism of the government."*

13

They both laughed, but then both cast their eyes quickly about their vicinity. No one seemed close enough to have evesdropped.

"Drink?" Rex said.

"No ,thanks, I don't drink."

He looked at her, his eyebrows up. "These days? What in the world do you do with your time?"

Her eyes went over him musingly. She took in his complexion, deeply tanned from the mountain skies, his figure, obviously in excellent trim. It was the second time within the hour that Rex Morris had borne the critical scrutiny of a beautiful woman.

She said, "By your appearance, you don't look as though you do too much bottle belting yourself, Techno . . ."

"Morris. Rex Morris."

"And you're from Taos? Good Howard, I wasn't listening, I'm afraid, when Lizzy introduced us. You must be the son of . . ."

He chimed in with her again and together they chanted, *"Leonard Morris."*

Rex said, "I'm beginning to get mighty tired of being my father's son."

She had new interest in her face and in her voice. "No, you're not," she said.

"No, I suppose not, really. He's not the sort of old boy that you can refrain from loving."

Paula Klein said, her voice little more than a whisper, "The question you asked. My grandfather was one of the very last to hold out against the religious amalgamations of the Temple."

"I see," Rex said uncomfortably.

She said, "He practiced one of the old religions until the end, though they demoted him to a common engineer." She added, her voice musing, "It takes time in our society today to live such a matter down."

Rex said uncomfortably, "I'm afraid it would be embarrassing if someone heard us, Techna Klein."

She looked at him strangely for a moment, but then

14

shook her head. "Look," she said, "how would you like to get out of this—and talk?"

He grinned. "Best proposition I've had all day."

"Follow me. I know this apartment of Lizzy's. There's a back way and nobody'll see us leave."

Rex Morris mentally shrugged. This cocktail party, like a dozen others he'd already attended under his uncle's wing, wasn't particularly significant. Uncle Bill was pulling the right strings, using his contacts to the best advantage. Some of the top hierarchy of the functional sequences and the Temple were here today, but Rex's appearance on the scene was not particularly necessary.

2.

Paula led the way, skirting the room, and finally disappearing through a door. They emerged into a sterile, white and chrome room with a good many cabinets, tables, and devices with which Rex wasn't familiar.

"What in the name of the Great Scott is this?" he said.

She said. "It's a kitchen."

"A *kitchen.* You mean where you cook food? In a private apartment, in this day and age?"

"Lizzy's a fiend for antiques," she said. "And a fiend for doing things the old ways. Come on, through here. It's a back entrance. A service entrance. I used to play here a great deal when I was a girl. Lizzy's husband was a dear —as she is, of course."

She led the way out a back door and to a service elevator. They stepped inside and Paula said, "Servo-term, please."

"Carried out Techna Klein."

She said to the mystified Rex, "It still remembers my identity after all these years."

The service elevator lowered them at sickening speed to two levels below ground. They issued into one of the building's servo-terms and Paula, still obviously knowing her way around, stepped over to a Transport Functional Sequence call box and dialed for a two passenger aircushion car.

16

In the way of conversation she said, "I imagine that in your part of the Technate there are still quite a few privately owned cars."

"Not as many as you'd think," Rex told her, as they waited. "Taos has an adequate Transportation FS garage. Of course, our house is about fourteen kilometers out of town so it takes time for delivery. But the trouble with owning your own is that you're so limited. Using the TFS garage services means you can use a fast sports model one day, an eight passenger limousine the next, a pick-up truck the following day, a four passenger sedan another time."

"Of course," Paula said. "My grandfather remembered when cars were commonly privately owned—except for taxis and rent-a-car services which were in their infancy then. He said the streets were so filled that you couldn't make headway except at a crawl, and that you couldn't find a place to park. It must have been before the underground, automated roads. Here we are."

A robo controlled air-cushion two seater had made its way down a ramp and now approached them. It slithered up to the curb next to where they stood and the door automatically opened.

Paula walked around to the other side and got in behind the manual controls. "I'll drive," she said. "I know the town better than you do."

Rex was mildly surprised that she didn't simply dial their designation. However, he said, "Look, where are we going?"

"You'll see," she chuckled. "My invitation was that we go someplace—and talk. Okay, we're going someplace—and talk." They entered the city's traffic at one of the lower levels and Paula set the dials.

Ten minutes later brought them to what was obviously the surface exit nearest to their destination, whatever that was. They issued into the city proper. Rex didn't recognize the location, which wasn't overly surprising since he had only been in town for a week. Not that he would have had much trouble finding it again. It was one of the less swank theatrical and nightclub-restaurant-bar centers.

17

Paula took over the manual controls again, drove for a few blocks, and then pulled up to the curb. They got out and she dismissed the car, to allow it to remain in traffic or at a parking pool until summoned again, and then led the way down a narrowish street.

Rex looked about him questioningly. "This must be one of the older streets in the city."

"I suppose so."

"Look, confound it, where are we going?"

She grinned at him mockingly. It was the first time he had seen her smile, really. Her smile came off big, and he had the sudden feeling that he wouldn't mind seeing her smile a great many times. She said, "You'll see, mister-son-of-Leonard-Morris."

He groaned.

They entered an averagely non-descript building, come down before the age of the high-rise, super-apartment buildings. Rex had at first decided that it was one of those largely devoted to effective class homes. However, if so, there were some strange elements. They walked along a corridor for a few yards and then took what seemed to be a service elevator. Two levels down, they emerged into a small, furnitureless room, and Paula stood before a tell-screen.

A voice said, "We recognize you, Paula Klein, but who is this stranger? He is not a member."

"I vouch for him," Paula said impatiently.

Rex Morris felt a stir of nervousness. Where was this leading? He didn't like it. He'd had no idea . . .

The voice said, "Obviously you vouch for him, or you wouldn't have brought him . . . However, Paula Klein, you know the rules of this establishment and this Techno class stranger is unknown to us."

She said impatiently, "I tell you, he is perfectly safe. And, as you very well know, I am Technician caste myself."

"But how do we know? I am sorry, sir, but this is a private establishment, and . . ."

Paula snapped, "This is Techno Rex Morris, son of

18

Hero of the Technate Leonard Morris. Now, is that enough for you?"

There was a long moment of silence.

Then the voice said, an element of apology there, "Welcome to this speakeasy, Techno Morris."

Paula snorted and led the way to where a heavy, padded door was sliding open.

"Speakeasy!" Rex blurted.

3.

She turned to him and her grin was mischievous and she had a certain air of triumph. "I told you—somewhere where we can talk. Where else is there in Greater Washington but a speakeasy?"

"Great Scott," Rex muttered.

Inside, there must have been at least a half dozen rooms of various sizes. Each of them, in turn, held half a dozen round tables. Rex was reminded, vaguely, of a poker table, only these were larger. Each table would comfortably seat a dozen or so. Some, however, had twice that number, seated or standing about it. Each table had at its center an autobar and possibly half of the club's attenders were sipping away at coffee or other beverages.

But drinking was obviously not the attraction.

"Come over here," Paula said to him, her dark eyes sparking. And then, under her breath, "There is only one fast rule. You're not to take exception to what anyone says—no matter how extreme. You're allowed to say anything you wish, but so is everyone else."

Rex Morris cleared his throat unhappily. "See here, I'd rather you wouldn't introduce me by name."

She looked at him oddly. "All right, but you can trust these people. They're in the same boat as you are. I gave your name out there in front just so we could get in.

20

From now on, you'd have no trouble if you ever wanted to return on your own." `

They had come up to a table, largely occupied by more elderly conversationalists. Most of these remained quiet, listening, possibly puffing on pipe or cigarette, or sipping coffee or beer. There was a relaxed atmosphere. Just at present, one was holding forth pronouncedly. He was a thin, sharply incisive, Senior Effective.

"My question is *why?*" he was saying. "Why, why— *why?* And nobody answers it. On the lower levels of religious belief we descend to the ridiculous. The argument gives us a supreme being, or beings, who create universe and man and then spend considerable time supervising him and usually making demands in the way of worship. If individual man is 'good,' upon death he is rewarded throughout all eternity; if he is 'bad' he is punished throughout all eternity. An obviously childish conception and originally born in primitive minds. On top of it all what is good and what is bad is usually arbitrarily decided upon by a priesthood." The speaker's voice was dry. "And often indeed their decisions on what is sin and what is righteous, are strongly influenced by their own material advantage."

One of his audience grunted at that point but it wasn't clear if it was assent or rejection.

The speaker turned to him. "Seldom does one find, throughout history, an organized religion's priesthood which had not managed to control considerable wealth. There are exceptions, but they are only exceptions, the rule stands. A religious movement might start out with dreamers and idealists who live in self-imposed poverty. Jesus and his immediate disciples are an example. But within a century or so, when the new religion has gained a multitude of followers, we find the new generation of religious leaders living on the fat of the land."

Another of the table's occupants said, "I think you're drifting away from your original point."

"No I'm not. My question, which I ask of all the religions, is *why?* On this lower level of personal gods the

21

situation is most obvious. God creates man, sets him some rather impossible regulations, especially in such instinctive matters as sex, and then punishes or rewards him according to how he reacts. But *why?* Why should an all powerful god go to such bother? The question is the same, however, on any level of religious thought. If there is a supreme being directing all this, what motivates him? To what end does he create such a foolish, pathetic creature as man?"

One of the older men took his pipe from his mouth and said softly, "The fact that we cannot answer your question doesn't mean there is no answer. Perhaps to the Deity the answer is a very obvious one. Perhaps, for some reason, he does not want us to know why he created us. Perhaps we are fated never to find out."

Rex Morris drew Paula Klein back a few yards from the table. His lips were dry. "Look here," he whispered, "if the Temple knew about this conversation, those men would be apprehended and would probably lose status. They might even be exiled from the Technate. Or . . . or even . . ."

"Be imprisoned or meet violence," Paula finished for him.

"Yes, that's what I mean," he said urgently.

"Well?" she said.

"I think we ought to get out of here."

She laughed softly. "I'm afraid the example your father set—among others—has swept the more intelligent citizens of our society. This is by no means the only speakeasy in Greater Washington. And every city has its quota."

"But what's the point? Sooner or later the Temple is going to crack down on these men. You simply can't *say* the sort of thing they're saying."

"It's not just the Temple. What controversial subjects, in particular are you interested in?"

"Me? Why, I . . ."

"Come on over here. If I know this chap, there at the table in the corner, you'll get a laugh.

22

Rex Morris rolled his eyes upward in protest but followed her grudgingly to the group she had indicated.

"Motherhood," a heavy-set, pale complexioned junior effective was sneering. "What is there about a mother that automatically makes her an object of veneration, adoration? Take a sloppy, half-baked, under-educated, mealy mouthed, objectionable kid of eighteen and let her forget to take her pills, or otherwise be caught with her prophylactic equipment malfunctioning. Nine months later and miracle of miracles, she's a veritable shrine at which to worship. She's a *mother!* Say anything against motherhood and the mob is screaming for your blood. Not that I hold any brief for the average father either. In my estimation, not one person in a hundred is capable of participating in raising the nation's young. They muddle through, untrained, incapable, being the product of the same sort of parents themselves. How we do as well as we do, is a mystery to me." He snorted his disgust and lapsed into temporary silence.

Paula said slyly, "Don't you love your own mother, Effective?"

He looked up at her and snorted again. "I *love* her, perhaps, but I also realize her shortcomings. God! how she suffers. What a martyr. How she has sacrificed through the years for her children. How cruel they all are, not to realize it and appreciate her. A typical example!"

Someone else at the table said, "If you think that parents are unsuitable for raising children, who would you substitute?"

"Trained professionals, of course. In the same manner that we seek out those who have an aptitude for being engineers, pilots, teachers, artists, or whatever, let us start out those who have an aptitude for raising children . . ."

Rex shook his head. "What's over there?" he whispered to Paula, nodding at a table that was not only full but had several standees around its perimeter of chairs.

"I wouldn't know," she whispered back. "The idea is just to drift around until you find something of interest. Then you either listen or join in, if you wish."

A minor debate was evidently underway, instead of a monologue.

One participant was saying doggedly, "I'm not narrow minded on the subject. I have no desire to burn homosexuals at the stake. If their . . . tastes . . . are different than mine, it's their own business." He leaned forward and pointed a finger at a younger man across the table from him. "However, such relations between consenting adults is one thing. But I think they should stick to themselves and to adults. I don't approve of their seducing young people who otherwise would remain normal."

"What in the world do you mean by normal?" the other said in disgust. "Define normal, as applied to sex, for me."

"You know what I mean. The basic reason for the sex act is to procreate. That's normal. When you start interfering with that end product, you begin striking at the race. When an homosexual leads an otherwise normal young man or woman into his or her own path, he interferes with that person having children and replenishing the earth, as the expression goes."

"That's ridiculous," the other said. "Did Kinsey live for nothing? It's well known that practically everybody has a touch of the homosexual in him. The race isn't in danger simply because everyone doesn't conform to average sexual practice. Did the Greeks of the Golden Age fail to reproduce themselves? Certainly not. As a matter of fact they had such a population explosion that they had to migrate to colonies all over the Mediterranean. And, as you know the practice of homosexuality was almost universal among the Ancient Greeks."

Red lights were flashing on the wall, and the room went momentarily still.

The last speaker groaned, "A raid! And me on probation from the last time I was caught."

Paula's eyes were darting about the room. Already, the speakeasy's membership was on its feet, milling about undecidedly. Voices, some shrill began calling back and forth. All was confusion. There was a sound of pounding in the distance, a door was evidently being forced.

24

Somebody yelled, "How do we get out of here? They're coming in by both front and rear doors!"

"Great Scott," Rex Morris blurted. "We're caught. I'll never get a decent appointment now."

Paula Klein looked at him strangely for a moment, then, "Look, follow me. Here, come through here."

He followed her through several rooms, back through a door into a small corridor beyond. Into a tiny office, furnished simply with a table and two straight chairs. Incongruously, there was a portrait of the Supreme Technician hanging on a wall.

Behind the desk was seated a middle aged, red faced man in the dress of a Senior Effective. His expression registered disgust now. "A raid," he said bitterly. "The second one this month. What's wrong with the SFS, their Technician trying to get a promotion? Hello Paula." He looked at Rex. "Who's this?"

Paula said urgently, "Mike, this is Leonard Morris' son. He's newly in town. You're right about Technician Matt Edgeworth. He's bucking for Prime Technician and trying to get as much publicity as possible. If he catches Rex in a speakeasy, he might throw the book at him. You know that. Besides, Rex isn't affiliated with a functional sequence as yet. He'd have no organization to go to bat for him if he gets into the Technacourt. Mike, you've got to do something.

Mike jerked his head in the direction of the other rooms from which Paula and Rex had just come. "Everybody in there thinks he has some particularly good reason not to get caught. Why should you get special treatment?"

"Mike, this isn't just anybody. It's Leonard Morris' son. If he gets taken, it will be broadcast on every station in the Technate. And it'll be just one more blow to his father and it seems to me the old man has taken enough blows from our society."

Mike was evidently a man of quick decision and quick action. He was on his feet.

"All right, through here. You're on the vulnerable side yourself, Paula."

He pulled open the door of a clothes closet.

"I've only used this two or three times. Possibly the police know about it. I don't think so. I don't even use it myself. It's for *real* emergencies. Good luck, Techno Morris."

Rex muttered back, "Thanks—Mike."

"Oh hurry, Good Howard!" Paula said.

There was a pounding of heavy footsteps in the corridor.

She had pushed aside two or three coats to reveal a small door beyond, so set within the wall as to escape easy notice. She pressed against it and it fell away inward, even as Mike closed the door behind them.

It was dark.

"A lighter?" she said in a low whisper. "I can't see my hand in front of my face."

He flicked his lighter and by its rays they made their way down an ultra-narrow passage. It debouched through a seemingly normal door into a corridor beyond. This hallway was lit.

Paula said, "I haven't the vaguest idea of where we are, or how we get out of here."

Rex said, "All we can do is explore. This would seem to be some sort of storage area. Hope we don't run into anybody."

They shortly found a stairway and ascended it. There didn't seem to be any elevators. Two floors up they entered the lobby of what was obviously a small hotel, obviously of senior effective and below ranking.

The hotel was recent enough to be fully automated so that there was no staff present, but two or three of whom were obviously residents looked up at them, in various degrees of surprise. It wasn't exactly the sort of place from which to expect a couple of Technician rank to materialize.

Paula and Rex ignored them and made their way to the front entrance. They stood in the door for awhile looking out.

In the street beyond were a half dozen or so SFS effectives under the orders of another of the security police of engineer's rank. They were obviously guarding the entrance to the speakeasy while other members of their force were conducting the raid inside. Five or six of their vehicles, some designed to hold prisoners, were parked strategically around. Pedestrians went by with their eyes directly to the front, ignoring completely that something out of the ordinary was going on. The art of fearing to become involved was well developed in the Technate.

Rex said, "What do you think? Should we go back into the hotel and sit down in the lobby until it's over?"

Paula Klein thought about it, biting her under lip. "No," she said. "They might find that secret door in Mike's closet and come through it. If they found us here, in Techno clothing, they'd know darn well that we were on the run from that speakeasy. We'll have to brazen it out. Come on, Rex, take my arm."

Trying to look nonchalant and as though their emerging from a lower caste hotel was the most normal thing in the world, Rex Morris and Paula Klein made their way out to the street, joined the other pedestrians as inconspicuously as possible and strolled on past the SFS men.

Or, at least, that had been their hope.

However, the engineer in command blinked suddenly, blurted something to his men and the whole contingent snapped to rigid attention. Paula nodded to them, and continued on the way as though nothing in the world had happened.

A hundred feet down the street, Rex, staring at her, said, "What in the name of Great Scott was all that about?"

Paula was biting her lip. She said, "Confound it. That fool saw me come out of the hotel with you."

"What of it? But what I want to know is, what was that salute bit? Instead of arresting us they acted as though we were big-wigs."

Paula was impatient, "Klein, Klein. Don't you recognize my name?"

Rex came to a halt and continued to stare at her. "You

27

mean that Warren Klein's your husband? The Prime Technician of the Security Functional Sequence?"

"Not my husband, my brother. Good Howard, he'll be furious. He's already warned me to stay out of speakeasies, in view of his position."

4.

In the morning, at breakfast, William Morris was slyly inquisitive. "We seem to, ah, have lost you at Lizzy's party. I thought you had wandered off with the Nadine Sims girl, but I noticed she was still dancing with Technician Edgeworth."

Rex was dialing turtle eggs and sea pork, toast, butter and coffee. "Uh huh. I went off with Paula Klein."

His uncle pursed his lips. "Paula Klein, eh? Well, nice girl. However, well . . ."

"However what?" Rex frowned at him.

"Well, frankly, quite a madcap, so I understand. She's quite her brother's, ah, despair. You seem to have a tendency for young ladies connected with the Security FS, Rex. Do you think that, ah, well . . ." he let his sentence go unfinished.

Rex accepted delivery of his food from the autotable, and poked at it. "Whale butter," he said. "Do you know, Dad raises real butter on our place near Taos."

"Real butter? Oh, come now. It's seldom that even the Prime Technicians serve real butter on their tables. I ate with one only last week. You mean *cow* butter? Has he connections with a zoo? Oh, now really, my dear boy."

"Goat butter," Rex said. "Dad's big joke these days is telling people he's the last of the ranchers. He has a milch

29

goat, one of the last three or four in the area. Makes quite a hobby of her. Lot of trouble getting suitable graze and all, but he has fun doing it."

"How antique," his uncle said, wide eyed. "I must tell Lizzy Mihm about it. She'll be green."

The robo said from the wall speaker, "Engineer Lance Fredrics of the Security Functional Sequence at the disposal of Technician William Morris and Techno Rex Morris."

William Morris' eyebrows rose. "Security? What in the world would a Security Engineer want with me?"

Rex said nervously, "Oh, oh."

The older man's eyes went to him. "There's something I should know?"

Rex put down his fork, looked his embarrassment at his older companion. "I'm afraid I've pulled a boner, Uncle Bill. I hope it doesn't jeopardize your position."

"Position? Don't be ridiculous. I'm retired. What are you talking about?"

"I went to a speakeasy yesterday, Uncle Bill. There was a raid by the SFS. I thought I got out, undetected, but evidently not. How bad a spot am I in?"

"A speakeasy! Not in town a week and you've already located yourself a speakeasy. By the Good Howard you're certainly walking in your father's footsteps!"

"I was taken to one. I've heard about such places before, of course but I'd never seen one. We don't have them out in the country. I suppose I should have left immediately, but I was curious."

William Morris cast his eyes upward. "Well, let's have the officer in and explain it all. However, I would think, Rex, that in view of your father's, ah, notoriety, that you'd be a bit more circumspect."

"Sorry, Uncle Bill."

His uncle raised his voice. "Show Engineer Fredrics in."

"Carried out," the robo voice said.

The door opened and a blank faced, stockily built Security FS uniformed Senior Engineer entered. He stopped

30

two feet within the doorway, clicked his heels and rapped, "Respects to Technician Morris."

"Oh, relax, relax," William Morris muttered. "Sit down, Fredrics. Would you like coffee? It's genuine coffee, from the South American Technate."

Engineer Fredrics was taken aback. "Genuine coffee?"

William Morris chuckled. "Well, from the Brazilian hydroponic tanks. You'll appreciate the fact that rank has its privileges, Fredrics. Ah, particularly after you secure your own appointment to the rank of Technician, eh?"

The Security man took a chair self consciously, and accepted the cup of coffee his host had dialed for him. He cleared his throat and said, "Yes, sir. Thank you. Uh, actually, it's Techno Morris I've been assigned to see."

The older man chuckled as he offered sugar and cream.

"So I understand. My nephew was just telling me he was inadvertently taken to a speakeasy, yesterday."

"Well, yes."

"Inadvertently," William Morris chuckled again. "Utter foolishness. I've already spoken to him about it."

Engineer Fredrics was embarrassed. "Well, sir, my orders were to pick Techno Morris up and . . ."

William Morris raised a hand and waved it in negation. "Don't bother, young man. I'll get in touch with your Technician and clear this all up."

Rex Morris spoke for the first time. "Uncle Bill, I don't want to hide behind you on this matter. I made a mistake and I'm willing to face up to it"

"Let me handle this, my boy. You're too new in town to be getting a bad name for yourself. It might jeopardize your receiving a suitable appointment." Uncle Bill turned to the security officer. "I suppose that Matt Edgeworth is your superior. I'll phone him right after breakfast."

Fredrics squirmed in his chair, sorry now that he hadn't been able to resist the invitation to coffee. It's difficult to deal in an official capacity with someone whose hospitality you are accepting. He said, "Sir, my orders are to bring Techno Morris into headquarters."

"Indeed?" the older Morris said coldly. "Perhaps you'd better have your Technician phone *me*, Engineer Fredrics. I am not at all sure I appreciate this cavalier treatment of my guest and relative."

The SFS man was on his feet again, his face flushed.

"Sir, Technician Edgeworth has been conducting a crackdown on speakeasies. The statistics show they've more than doubled in the past year. The Technician was indignant this morning when he learned that Techno Morris, hardly in town more than a few days, was already seen in one. The implication is that he is untouchable because of his family's prominence."

"I told you that my nephew was taken to this place without his knowledge. It was not his fault."

"Taken by whom?" The Security officer was standing firm.

Rex blurted, "I don't mind telling you that. I object to these places and don't mind cooperating at all. I was taken by Techna Paula Klein."

"Rex. . . !" his uncle said.

"Paula Klein?" the officer said blankly.

There was a long moment of uncomfortable silence. Finally Senior Engineer Lance Fredrics clicked his heel again. "I'll report to my superior. Technician Morris, my respects. May I have permission to leave?"

"Certainly."

Before turning to make his retreat, the Security officer shot a quick glance at Rex Morris. There was faint contempt in it.

When he was gone, William Morris said uncomfortably, "Did you think that was necessary, Rex? Paula is a bit on the wayward side, but she is a fine girl."

Rex shrugged and buttered another piece of toast. "What difference will it make to her with her brother Prime Technician of Security? Everything will take care of itself. This nosy Technician Edgeworth wouldn't dare involve a member of his superior's family in a scandal."

"Perhaps," his uncle said, still uncomfortable.

Rex said, "See here, how did they know I was at that speakeasy? We seemingly escaped."

"Was it an effective caste place?"

"Why, I suppose so. We seemed to be the only Technicians present. There were one or two engineers."

The older man grunted disgust. "Those effective caste speakeasies are riddled with police. Nothing is said, nothing goes on that isn't reported."

"But then why are they tolerated? Why doesn't this Technician Edgeworth close them all up with one big series of raids?"

"Probably because a known evil that you can keep track of is better than an unknown one. The Security FS knows that a certain element of the population is going to discuss controversial subjects come what may. It's better to keep track than to try and suppress completely. When some individual goes too far, becomes downright subversive, he's picked up and dealt with."

Rex shook his head unbelievingly. "Well, all I can say is that I can see where the Technate's best brains, as represented by the Supreme Technician himself and such high ranking officials as you Prime Technicians and Technicians might find it necessary to discuss controversial matters, but I can't see it being allowed anyone beneath, say, Senior Engineer's rank, at the very lowest."

His uncle grunted. "That's the way it goes, my boy. Everybody seems to think that *he* shouldn't be abridged in his thinking or his speech, but that everyone below his rank should."

"Uncle Bill," Rex Morris said, evidently shocked. "You must be joking."

His uncle grunted cynically again. "However, next time you want to take in a speakeasy, don't go to one of those lower caste ones. They exist on all levels, my boy; Effective, Engineer, and Technician. When the urge hits you, let me know."

The eyes of the younger man widened. "You mean, you belong to one yourself?" He looked quickly about the room.

William Morris chuckled. "No microphones, no bugs,

Rex. Certainly you must realize that one of the privileges of my rank, even though I'm retired, is that there is no monitoring of my home. You're as free here as in a speakeasy, and considerably safer."

5.

Rex said, "Well, of course, I realize that rank has its privileges."

His uncle was obviously still nettled by the Security Engineer who had intruded upon his privacy. He said, "Yes, but I'm afraid that even they are being eroded away in what has become a truly naked society, a society without privacy. When the early founders of the Technate took their initial steps against non-conformists, I wonder if they ever expected to go this far."

"Uncle Bill!"

"Oh, don't be such a ninny, my boy. It's one thing, watching yourself at a place like one of Lizzy Mihm's parties, but I'm your uncle and here we are in the privacy of my home. We are both members of the Technician caste. If we can't discuss serious matters, who can?"

"Well . . ." Rex Morris shifted in his chair uncomfortably. "I've always been so conscious of Dad's unorthodox viewpoints that I suppose possibly I've swung to the opposite extreme."

The older man wasn't particularly listening. He said, a musing quality in his voice, "I wonder where it all began. We Americans, in the infancy of our country, prided ourselves upon being so open, so outspoken. Did you know that even the secret ballot was scorned in the early days of the American Republic?"

"Secret ballot?" Rex said vaguely, and obviously not very interested.

"In early post-revolution America, when they held an election, the voters—all men, of course, in those days, and all property holders—usually came down to the village square. The candidates would be there and usually a table where a clerk would register the votes as cast. Each voter would step forward and cast his vote verbally. The candidate for whom he voted would thank him and it would be tabulated. Each man was proud to cast his vote and didn't give a damn who knew for whom he stood. The secret ballot came in later, when citizens began to be afraid to let their boss, their neighbors, or whoever, know how they had voted, for fear that they might become discriminated against as a result."

Rex yawned and said, "What a ridiculous manner in which to select a nation's rulers. Voting." He poured himself a final cup of coffee.

William Morris was squinting thoughtfully. He mused, "I can remember my grandfather telling about the nature of people when he was a lad. In the 30s, when you drove across country there were large numbers of hitchhikers, as they called them. People who had no cars of their own and wanted rides. Invariably they were picked up. It didn't occur to motorists not to pick them up. As times became more affluent and the current depression ended, the hitchhiker disappeared. As they grew more affluent, people thought they had more to lose, they became afraid of robbery, of not being insured in case of accident, that sort of thing. They wouldn't dream of picking up a young traveler, or somebody too poor to own his own car."

Rex stirred his coffee.

His uncle said, "A callous attitude grew. The old virtues eroded. I remember reading of a young girl being murdered in New York, a murder that took place over a period of at least an hour. More than thirty persons heard her cries but none even went so far as to phone the police. They didn't want to become involved, as they called it. They might have been required to go down to the police station, or testify in court. So they allowed a neighbor to be done to death, to avoid that. Other people were robbed or beaten by criminals in the subways or streets, and none would come to their assistance—for fear of becoming involved."

Rex said lazily, "What's all this got to do with avoiding controversial questions?"

"It's related, I suppose. It's all part of the evolution of the gutless wonder, the modern American. Don't rock the boat. Don't say anything that might cause umbrage. Avoid politics and religion in your discussion, no matter how much they cry to be discussed. Talk about wishy-washy things."

"Makes for easier living," Rex murmured, sipping at his coffee.

"Is easier living what we must strive for, Rex? Your father doesn't think so."

"Oh, *Dad,*" Rex snorted.

His uncle was still musing. "But that wasn't all. The avoiding of the controversial. It must have been the Cold War that finally brought it to a head. The Dies Committee, the Un-American Activities Committee, and finally Senator McCarthy's era. Everybody became so frightened of being branded a Red that they were afraid to open their mouths on any subject controversial. It got to the point where if you wore slightly unorthodox clothes, were an atheist or an agnostic, or even grew a beard, you were looked at askance."

"A beard!" Rex snorted again. "Great Scott!"

His uncle looked at him. "It was the way nature designed us, my boy. Nature adorns man with a beard."

Rex laughed as though in protest. "Well, then, it's one place were we've improved on nature."

William Morris went back to worrying his theme. "But I suppose it was the coming of the miniturized bug that finished us off. That and the National Data Banks and every citizen having a dossier into which every vital bit of information about him was recorded by the computers. His vital statistics, including his criminal record, if any, his medical record, his data pertaining to the Internal Revenue Department, his credit rating, his I.Q. and other

37

educational data. From cradle to the grave, everything that pertains to you goes into your dossier. All phone calls are monitored, in this naked society of ours, and if there is any reason, whatsoever, the Security Functional Sequence has the ability to bug any room, any car, any public restaurant or other meeting place. They have the ability to pick up your conversation from half a mile away, even though you are walking along the street. No wonder our people, with this hanging over their heads every moment of their lives, are circumspect in everything they say."

Rex put down his cup and yawned again. "Well, Uncle Bill, you've got to admit it leads to a stable society."

"That it does," his uncle said. His eyes narrowed a bit. "I wouldn't want it any other way, of course."

"Of course not." Rex chuckled in deprecation. "If the whole country has never had it so good, why should we of the Technician caste, on top of the heap, have any complaints? Great Scott, not even the effectives, on the bottom, have any complaints."

The older man said, his voice slightly changed, "I wouldn't expect you to repeat this conversation, my boy."

Rex Morris' eyebrows went up. "Uncle Bill! You think I want to stick my neck out, the way Dad does? Why, this kind of talk I wouldn't carry on with my wife, if I had one. All I can say is that you and Dad must have some sort of gene in your make-up that can't be kept down." He laughed and added, "Thank goodness it seems to have missed me. Or, perhaps, I should say, thank Mother. She seems to have bred it out of me."

The older Morris grunted and changed the subject, evidently uncomfortable now that he had carried it as far as he had. He said, "What's on the program today, my boy?"

Rex Morris tossed his napkin into the table disposal chute and came to his feet. "Oh, I think I'll wander around town a bit and get the feel of it. You've been hurrying me about from one party to the next so fast that I haven't been able to see anything except the apartments of your friends."

38

"You can't attend too many parties, in your position, Rex. It's where the contacts are made. Greater Washington is a city of parties. I'd wager more decisions on national policies, national production and promotion or demotion of key personnel are made at such get-togethers than are in the offices."

"After observing the way you do things in this town for only one week, I suspect you're right," Rex said humorously. "What amazes me is that the whole Technician caste doesn't have a perpetual hangover."

"Lay it all to progress, my boy. The new sober-up pills are the greatest invention since the wheel."

6.

The Technate of North America consisted of an amalgamation of the former Canada, United States, Mexico, the Caribbean Islands and the Central American nations down to and including Panama. Established in the latter part of the twentieth century, it was an internally self-sufficient, collectivized society requiring neither foreign sources of raw materials nor markets for surplus commodities.

The developments of the second industrial revolution in science, in industry, in practically all fields of endeavor, had solved the problem of the production of abundance. The government of the Technate solved those of distribution. The lowliest citizen commanded from the cradle to the grave not only the necessities of life but many of its luxuries. It was an affluent society beyond the dreams of the Utopians.

The government itself was a self perpetuation hierarchy. Recommendation from below and appointment from above, was the formula.

At the peak was the Supreme Technician, head of the Congress of Prime Technicians and carrying a veto power over its decisions. His position held for life and upon his demise the Prime Technicians elected from their number a new incumbent of the office.

Such an election was the sole example of the democratic process in the Technate society, for it had been in complete rejection of the democratic principle that the Technate had come to power. Democracy, it had been decided, was inefficient in the modern world. It led to graft, corruption and invariably to the power of inept politicians whose efforts were directed at gaining office for the office's sake. Political parties had become a disgrace by the middle of the 20th century, elections a farce; in another generation they had become a dangerous farce.

Ranking head, then, of the Technate was the Supreme Technician who was elected from and by the twenty-five man body of the Congress of Prime Technicians. Upon the death or retirement of a member of this ruling body, a new member was appointed from the ranks of the next lower echelon, the Technicians of the Functional Sequence of the industry the demised Prime Technician had headed.

For each Prime Technician was the titular head of one of the Technate's Functional Sequences such as Transport, Communications, Education, Medicine, Entertainment, Construction—or Security. The work of the Congress of Prime Technicians was to plan the Technate's production and distribution and to coordinate the efforts of the twenty-five different Functional Sequences. It was a planning body, rather than a legislative or judicial one.

Below each Prime Technician was a varying number of Technicians, according to the make-up of the individual Functional Sequence. Obviously they differed somewhat since the Communications Functional Sequence would have other problems than, say, those of the Entertainment Functional Sequence or of Medicine. The Technician was the official in charge of all activity in a given geographical area. For instance, a Technician might be in complete command of the Entertainment FS for the West Coast, another for the Middle West, another for the area once known as Mexico.

The formula was recommendation from below, appointment from above. When a Prime Technician died or retired, the Technicians under him recommended from their ranks a candidate for the office. The Congress either appointed this candidate or rejected him and called for another recommendation.

And so it went all the way down the line. Below the Technicians were the Senior Engineers, below them the Junior Engineers. Then came the big drop to Senior Effective, Junior Effective and, at the bottom of the pyramid, the Effective.

Recommendation from below, appointment from above.

From the first nepotism and favoritism were the rule. When a man is in a position to appoint others to power and privilege he is hard put to ignore his children, his relatives, his friends.

A new aristocracy arose, a new class in a society that supposedly was classless—there had been societies before that had claimed to be classless. The Technate system differed possibly from class divided society in the past when basically upper classes differed from lower ones in their enjoyment of the material products of their culture, but the Techno class was still an upper one, the Engineers a middle, and the Effective class a lower one. Food, clothing, shelter, medicine, education and entertainment there were for all aplenty—but there are other things than these, for man does not live on bread alone.

A society whose direction is based on nepotism and favoritism is apt to be a static society. When one is born to the purple, rather than achieving it through his own superior efforts, he is apt to have small ability for the office. Why strive, when the goal is effortlessly achieved?

Such a society is also apt to be ultra-conservative for no crown is less easy than an undeserved one.

The trend toward conformism had started even before the advent of the Technate. The tendency accelerated under it. Until eventually . . .

7.

Rex Morris left the 185th floor terrace apartment of his uncle and crossed to the elevator banks. The screen of the elevator for which he headed picked him up and the door opened.

There was no one else in the compartment. Rex stepped inside and said, "175th floor, please."

"Carried out, Techno Morris," a robo voice answered. The door smoothly closed again and the compartment began to drop.

Rex marveled, all over again, at the efficiency of the high-rise apartment building in which his uncle made his home. When he had first appeared on the scene, fresh from his Western home, his uncle had introduced him to the automated reception desk in the lobby and from then on the computer connected screens at the entrance, on the elevator banks, and at his uncle's door all recognized him and passed him. He knew, however, that there were limitations on his movements, as there were on those of anyone else in the 200 floor high-rise apartment building which contained in all, counting all three towers, more than ten thousand apartments.

In the way of experimentation, he had once requested the elevator to take him to the 65th floor. Within seconds a voice had said, "Techno Rex Morris, your residence is on the 185th floor. What is your purpose in stopping at

43

the 65th floor? If you are visiting someone on that floor will you please reveal his name so that we may check if you are expected?"

Rex had thought, "I'll be damned. I'd hate to have to try and burglarize this building." But aloud he said, "Oh yes, excuse me. I was thinking about something else. 185th floor, please."

"Carried out," the robo voice said.

On the 175th floor he left the elevator and crossed the corridor to the express banks and took another. Once again, there was no one else in it.

He said, "Ground floor, and bent his knees slightly to accommodate to the accelerated drop. He still wasn't really used to the speed of these confounded things.

Sometimes he wondered at the anthill-like life led by the citizens in this day's cities. There must be some forty thousand residents in this building, and few indeed had the spacious quarters his uncle could boast. On the lower levels, of course, the effective caste apartments were small in the extreme, especially those occupied by singles or even couples without children. Mini-apartments, they called them, and though wonders of efficiency and compactness, Rex Morris shuddered at the thought of residing in one. Now, he gave a sigh for the single level, adobe and viga construction, of his father's home in the part of the Technate once known as New Mexico.

On the ground floor he stepped out into the lobby devoted to the Technician caste residents of this tower of the high-rise and for the first time since leaving William Morris' apartment ran into fellow Technos. They were clad alike in Technician gray, the badge of his class which set them off immediately from either engineers or effectives. Most seemed somewhere important bent, and were obviously off for this part of the day's shift to offices, laboratories, schools or wherever.

Rex didn't envy them. He suspected that not one in five worked at a job he really liked. Under the Technate, a member of the Technician class got an appointment in a field where he had connections and pull, not necessarily in some Functional Sequence in which he was interested in the work. Rex sometimes wondered if the lowly effective, whose position was largely decided by ability, wasn't happier in his work.

He strode out the luxurious marble entrance and hesitated for a moment on the steps. He had decided to stroll around the center-city, still largely devoted to the governmental buildings and monuments of yesteryear. The old Washington had been preserved almost in its entirety, a virtual museum. For that matter, the White House was still the official residence of the Supreme Technician, although the story was that he spent precious little time there.

He looked out in the direction of the Washington Monument and decided it was too far to walk. He considered taking the escalator down to the lower levels and zipping over in one of the twenty-seater hover-jets, but decided against it. He wasn't in that much of a hurry, and, in actuality had a certain horror of the automated, underground roads which had largely solved the problems of traffic and parking which had formerly plagued the country.

Instead, he made his way to the nearest Transportation Functional Sequence box and dialed a one-seater floater, open air.

When it smoothed up to the curb he stepped in and murmured, "The Washington Monument." As a member of the Techno caste it wasn't necessary for him to utilize his Universal Credit Card. It had long since been decided by the powers that were that it was more efficient to provide free transportation for all of Technician standing, so that they wouldn't have to be bothered by such mundane things.

A robo voice said, "Carried out," and the small hover car edged into the light traffic and took off through the wooded parks which surrounded the apartment building and toward the obelisk-like monument to the first president of the then United States.

All heavy traffic as well as all traffic that was in a hurry, was on the underground level, of course, and hence here above there were precious few vehicles, particularly at this time of day. Later on, there would be more

45

children in the playgrounds, more pedestrians out to sample the air, more young people, walking hand in hand, as young people have walked in every age since Og the Caveman first sparked his, to him, beautiful mate to be.

Rex Morris was in no great hurry. Not that it would have done him much good if he was. Street traffic operated at a twenty-five kilometer an hour maximum speed, save for official and police vehicles. Automobile accidents were a thing of the past.

Yes, traffic was light. In fact, he noted but one car behind him as his own vehicle emerged from the park which surrounded his uncle's apartment house and entered that of the next high-rise. The other car was also a one seater, and Technician gray in color.

At the monument, he decided against getting out and instructed his vehicle to circle it. It came to him, in humor, that this monument to The Father of His Country, was well selected. It was a copy of an obelisk, the Egyptian phallic symbol.

He instructed the car to circle the White House, and like a score of millions of tourists before him, goggled at the source of so much American history. However, something was nagging away at the back of his mind. He couldn't quite put his finger on it.

He shrugged and had the car take him to the Ford Theatre, where long ago Lincoln had acted out his tragedy with Booth. The place was now a museum and he left the car to enter. And then it came to him, for a block behind another car pulled up to the curb. A one seater which was painted a Technician gray.

Possibly it was coincidence. But now he realized that the other small vehicle had been following him since he left his uncle's apartment house. He frowned. Of course, it was possible that the other was on exactly the same mission as was Rex Morris. That is, he was simply sightseeing, and just about any Greater Washington sightseer would pick the same places as had Rex—however, it was somewhat unlikely that he would have visited them in the same order.

Rex Morris walked over to look at the billboard, replicas of the same ones that had graced the theatre front on the night of tragedy. He stood there, looking up, but from the side of his eyes checked the other car. It was parked, but no one had left it. If the occupant had been a tourist, interested in seeing the Ford Theatre, it would be expected that he would have driven closer and then emerged.

Rex got back into his own car and directed it to the Smithsonian Institute. He found an excuse to look back without being obvious. There was no doubt at all about it. He was deliberately being followed. Why? He had no idea.

On a sudden impulse, he had the car stop before an effective caste autobar.

He said, even as he left it, "I won't require you any further."

"Carried out," the robo voice said and his vehicle started up and merged back into the traffic, heavier by this hour and in this part of the city than it had been earlier.

Rex Morris approached the door of the bar. The door screen picked him up and the door slid aside. He entered and looked about. It was seldom that he entered an effective caste place. It wasn't usually done. The theory was that the presence of a Technician caste customer made the usual habituees uncomfortable—as though an admiral had entered an establishment usually frequented by ordinary seamen. Effectives and engineers sometimes blended a bit, and sometimes engineers, and especially senior engineers, and Technicians, but Technicians and effectives had far too little in common for them to cross categories and mingle to any extent.

The place was typical. Clean, sterile, large Tri-Di screens on the walls, screens large enough that the actors were portrayed life-size. At least fifty autotables of varying size were scatttered about. At this time of the day, there weren't more than a half dozen or so imbibers present.

Rex Morris made his way directly to the far side of the room and took a small table facing the door. He looked at the drink list, put his Universal Credit Card in the table slot and dialed himself a glass of beer, which he didn't actually want. The center of the table sank down to return almost immediately with a tall ten ounce glass and its brownish contents.

The street door opened and a newcomer entered. He was an empty faced, burly type who could have played a wonderful stereotype villain on any Tri-Di show. He was dressed inconspicuously in standard effective caste wear. He didn't look in Rex Morris' direction but took a table near the door and studiously took in the drink list, finally reaching a decision and dialing.

Rex still didn't know.

A door in the rear of the autobar opened and an anxious little man, in junior effective garb, either rubbing his hands together in apprehension, or shaking with himself, scurried in Rex Morris' direction. He brought himself up next to Rex's table.

He said, "Yes, sir."

Rex looked up at him and fell into the mannerisms of the haughty aristocrat down through the ages; the Roman patrician, the Prussian *Junker,* the Russian Boyar, the British Lord. The high nostrils, the disdainful air.

"Yes . . . what?"

The other bobbed apologetically and made a slight gesture as though indicating his customer's gray suit, the gray suit of the Technician class.

"Yes, sir. I thought perhaps you had made an error. This is only an effective caste establishment, uh, sir."

"I know it's an effective caste bar, my good fellow," Rex said wearily. "Do you think me an idiot? However, my feet are tired, do you understand? And I simply refuse to go a step further until I've sat down awhile."

"Yes, sir, of course." the other hesitated unhappily. "Sir, there's a Technician bar, very nice, so I hear, just down the street one and a half blocks. Very swanky, sir, so I understand."

"I'm sure it is. See here, my good fellow, do I understand you are asking me to leave?"

The other was shocked. "Oh, *no,* sir. Of course not.

48

It's just that, well, the boys who, uh, hang out here are mostly junior effectives and effectives, and I guess that they might feel a little, uh, uncomfortable, you being here."

"Well then, let them leave." Rex Morris swept the room with his eyes, superciliously. "I don't seem to note any extreme distress. Great Scott, how can my sitting here resting my swollen feet and sipping a glass of this atrocious beer bother anyone?"

"Well, yes sir." The other bobbed again and scurried off to return to his inner office, or whatever the room was from which he had emerged.

Rex snorted, took a sip of his drink, then ostentiously took a look at his watch. He came to his feet and strolled toward what was obviously the men's room. He could feel eyes on his back.

Inside the men's room, he waited, standing to one side of the door. Long minutes passed.

Twice, others entered. On both occasions, Rex Morris went through the motions of being present on legitimate drinker's business until the newcomer left. Then he returned to his stance near the door. If he was correct in his suspicions, the other must be getting nervous about his long absence and wondering if there was a rear entry through which Rex might have left.

In his right pocket he had in his hand the heavy clasp knife he had carried since boyhood. It filled his grip, giving weight and bulk to his fist.

At long last the other came. The burly one who had entered the autobar after Rex.

His reaction was betraying. He started, to see Rex there at his post next to the door. His eyes flickered and he made a quick shuffle backward. Too late. The automated door had closed behind him. He began to bring his hands up defensively.

Too late, again. Rex slugged him against the jaw and the other staggered backward, dazed, Rex moved in quickly and slugged him again. The man collapsed forward, came to his knees shaking his head. He was a brute. Refusing to go out. He made a gurgling noise in his throat.

Rex Morris put everything into the next blow. Every ounce of his weight. The man collapsed forward onto his face.

Rex shot a look at the door, then knelt quickly and began going through the stranger's clothing. He came up with a wallet, opened it hurriedly, came out with the other's Universal Credit Card. It was on thick white plastic, Senior Effective caste, in short, and his Functional Sequence was Security.

Rex, in disgust, rammed the card back into the wallet and returned it to the fallen man's pocket.

He came to his feet and stared down, thinking rapidly. Great Scott, this was all he needed. Why had he been such an ass as to attack the man? After this morning's experience with Engineer Fredrics, he might have deduced than anyone following him must be from Security. But he'd had to be sure. At this stage of the game, he couldn't take the chance of there being unknowns.

He came to a sudden decision. Checked the man's condition. Decided the other would be out for at least another five minutes. Swung on his heel and left.

He marched indignantly to the door from which the establishment's manager had emerged earlier, stood there before the identity screen and snapped, "I demand some attention out here!"

One or two of the place's habitues, seated nearby, looked over at him but he ignored them, making a great show of indignation. The door opened and the timid soul was there and immediately began bobbing.

Rex glared at him. "What sort of an establishment *is* this?"

"Yes, sir. Uh, yes sir. What seems to be the trouble? The beer? I don't want to seem controversial but sometimes the beer ain't what . . ."

"The beer, indeed!" Rex Morris' ire increased. "Do you realize what just happened to me in your filthy restroom?"

The other stared at him in complete astonishment. His Adam's apple bobbed. "Well, no sir . . . What?"

"I was attacked by a pervert, or a footpad, or whatever he might turn out to be."

"Attacked?" The little man's eyes were bugging.

"Exactly! Thank heavens I was able to defend myself. I demand that you immediately notify the Security Functional Sequence and have the wretch arrested and brought before the Technocourt."

Rex Morris spun on his heel and stalked for the door.

8.

Rex Morris had first become aware of the fact that his father was considerably different than most fathers when he was in his early school years. They lived in a small hamlet named Arroyo Seco, fourteen kilometers out of the city of Taos. That in itself was on the non-conformist side, since surely Arroyo Seco was one of the last small hamlets in the Technate of America. With the advent of the high-rise apartments and all the advantage of that type life's efficiency, who would care to be so far out as to live in a single house?

Of course, Leonard Morris, as the ranking bio-chemist of his time, was expected to be a bit unusual. However, it could be carried to the extreme even when one was a Hero of the Technate.

So far back that he couldn't remember, young Rex had fallen into the not unusual youthful curiosity about adult conversation. In fact, he doted upon it. Nothing pleased him more than to sit silently listening to his father and mother at adult talk, covering matters often far beyond his ken.

As he grew older he began to realize that his presence sometimes put a damper on various fascinating subjects and even discovered that they were able to talk over his head, on requirement, using little code words or innuendoes he didn't comprehend. It was an irritant to the inquisitive youngster.

But youth isn't as improvident as all that. Leading off the living room cum library of the Morris home was a small chamber which was Rex's own and off-limits to adults, with the sole proviso that he keep it clean himself. Once a month or so his mother looked in to give it a routine check and always found the den spotless. Rex wasn't about to lose his retreat through neglect. The room abounded, of course, with Tri-Di photos of his current sports or entertainment heroes, with bows and arrows, boomerangs, a compressed air rifle, sports equipment of a dozen types, collections of everything from Indian arrowheads to butterflies. It also held a small table to work upon, two folding chairs and an old style army cot.

While he was still in the vicinity of ten years of age, Rex found that if he stationed himself on his cot near the door, stretched out upon it as though he was reading, and left the door open a crack, he could pick up unbeknownst most of the conversation that went on in the large living room. And for a period of years he had a positive addiction to eavesdropping. His conscience hurt him not at all. Face reality, early youth has no ethical code; that comes later in life—if ever.

Not that he could follow a great deal of what his father said, particularly when he was speaking to colleagues on matters scientific, or sometimes with friends on subjects involving political-economy and current affairs. After his mother passed away, young Rex Morris found that most of his father's conversation was over his head. It was an irritant. Adult talk had always sounded so fascinating!

However, young Rex developed a quirk, an eidetic memory of his father's words; all but total recall. Thus it was, somewhat later in life, he could bring back whole sentences of the older Morris' conversations, arguments and polemics with little effort. Discussions that had been beyond him, when originally entered into, were more understandable a few years or more later.

One day he had been in his room with the door closed and had been working on a model of a space satellite,

53

deeply concentrating to the point that he hadn't realized that his father had a visitor. Finally, he tossed his tools aside, came to his feet and crossed to the door with the intention of going into the auto-kitchen and dialing himself a sandwich.

His hand on the door, he halted. He could hear his father in the next room, speaking in heat. If there was anything that fascinated Rex Morris at the age of ten, it was adults in argument.

He left the door open a crack, selected a diagram of plans for model construction, stretched out on the cot and innocently began to study it, one ear cocked.

Leonard Morris was saying, "Of course it was a revolution. It was one of the most basic social revolutions the world has ever seen."

Another voice—Rex recognized it as that of Mike Wheaton, a friend from Taos—demurred. "Revolution is a somewhat controversial word, Leonard. The authorities prefer to think of the establishment of the Technate as evolution, rather than revolution."

The scientist snorted contempt of that. "Controversial words, controversial words! For the love of God, how can a word be controversial? *Ideas* can be controversial, but words are merely tools to convey ideas. How this confounded tendency ever began, I'll never know. It seems to have started as far back as the middle of the 20th century. All of a sudden terms such as socialist, left, communism, propaganda, Marxism, agitator, revolution, and such became dirty words to which one reacted automatically and negatively without thought. You could no longer discuss such subjects because a mental iron curtain went down as soon as the *words*—not the reality behind them—were used."

Wheaton's voice came again, unhappily. "Be that as it may, Leonard, the achievement of the Technate was peaceable and . . ."

"Who said it wasn't!"

"Well, you used the term revolution."

"A revolution doesn't have to be violent."

There was a silence.

54

Leonard Morris spoke up again. "A revolution simply means a basic socio-economic change. It may, but it doesn't necessarily involve violence. For instance, what socio-economic system prevailed in England, say, in the 16th century?"

"Why feudalism, I suppose."

"And what socio-economic system did England have by the 19th century?"

The other's voice came hesitantly, "Why, capitalism, I suppose."

"Very well, then when did the revolution take place? Revolution in the sense of the French Revolution or the Bolshevik Revolution in Russia? Or even the American Revolution of 1776?"

"Why, why I don't know."

"It didn't!" the older Morris said triumphantly. "The revolution came about but over a period of time, piece by piece, and so did the establishment of the Technate here in North America. It could have been foreseen a half a century earlier by anyone who cared to pry into the subject."

"Hindsight is always easier," the other said dryly.

Young Rex Morris, in the adjoining room, was getting an earful but only about half of it was understandable at his age. He squirmed, but didn't budge from his vantage point. He had the feeling that his father was winning the debate, but then, Rex was prejudiced.

Leonard Morris was launching full into his subject, now. He said, "Classical capitalism began to fall apart when the primary and secondary occupations fell off and the tertiary and quaternary occupations began to account for the majority of persons employed."

"You miss me there."

The scientist said impatiently, "The primary occupations are those of mining, agriculture, forestry, hunting, fishing. Secondary occupations are those that process the products of primary occupations, and tertiary are those that render services to the first two occupations."

"Well, what in the name of Great Scott are quaternary occupations?"

"Those that render services to tertiary occupations, or to each other. In actuality, that is the type occupation we of the Technician caste now hold down under the Technate. Occupations among the various agencies of government, the professions, the non-profit groups, very top management, higher education, that sort of thing."

"And you think the coming of this type of occupation was a revolutionary change?"

"Of course it was. Under classical capitalism, the entrepeneur was in charge of his enterprise. He prospered, or fell, according to his own abilities. It was a dog eat dog social system, but, then, most are. They had nicer words for it such as private enterprise, or free enterprise, but it was as ruthless a socio-economic system as has ever come down the pike—until, possible our own arrived."

"Oh now, Leonard."

"I mean it."

"Well, you'd better not let the word get around to the Security Functional Sequence."

"That's one of the reasons I say our society is even more ruthless. At least in most of the Western countries, including our own, you had freedom of speech and the press in the old days. You could say anything you damn well pleased. Most certainly you could in the privacy of your home."

"Well,"—the other was uncomfortable again—"back to this so-called revolution."

"It began, I suppose, about the time of the Second World War. Corporations became so large that individuals were no longer competent to run them, in the sense that Henry Ford was once absolute dictator of his industry, or John D. Rockerfeller his. They called it the Managerial Revolution, sometimes the New Industrial State. Over in England, an economist called it the rise of Meritocracy. In short, a new group emerged that managed and controlled industry but didn't own it. The old rich, who did own it, in spite of soaring inheritance, income and corporation taxes, through their domination of stock, were no longer a necessary element in society, and were rapidly losing power.

Rex Morris, still all ears, didn't understand that but he was becoming aware of the fact that his father's words didn't exactly conform with what he was already learning in school. He was becoming vaguely apprehensive. Leonard Morris shouldn't be talking this way—even to an old friend such as Mike Wheaton whom Rex has in youthful perceptiveness decided was a bit on the pompous side.

The scientist was saying, "The Meritocracy took over as the corporations became ever larger. By the middle of the 20th century two hundred corporations produced half of all the goods and services that were annually available in the United States and held two thirds of all assets involved in manufacturing. The fifty largest held over a third of all such assets. And only three, Standard Oil of New Jersey, General Motors and Ford had more gross income than all the farms in the country combined. The revenues of General Motors alone were eight times those of the State of New York, and slightly less than one fifth those of the Federal government.

"And this was just the beginning. Every year that went by saw the merging of these largest corporations, until, finally, for all practical purposes all industry and services were in the hands of a handful of supercorporations and they, in turn, in the hands of the Meritocracy, if you wish to call it that."

"You call that a revolution?" Wheaton scoffed.

"Yes. Or, at least, eventually it grew into one. At the same time, the government, with its own type of Meritocracy—I'm talking about the real government, the career officials, not the often nincompoops elected ones—was taking over an increasing amount of direction of the economy. Education, relief, polution control, husbanding of national resources, medicine, were taken out of the hands of local government and local enterprise. In a matter of a few decades, we found that the Federal government and the giant corporations were in complete control of the economy, and both were in the hands of the New Class, if you want to call them that—the Meritocracy, those who achieved to their position of power through

57

their ability, not through the inheritance of wealth or status. It didn't take long for the Technate to evolve."

Wheaton was still argumentive. "All right, if you want to call it a revolution. I guess it's largely a matter of definitions. However, I got the original opinion that you opposed our present way of doing things. From the way you sound now, you're all in favor of it."

There was amusement in Leonard Morris' voice now. "Oh, there's not much point in opposing history. It's too late to change it. My big point is, it's time now for another revolution."

"What!" his friend gasped. "Are you insane, saying things like *that?"*

But Leonard Morris often said things like *that,* as young Rex increasingly discovered. And as he grew older it increasingly distressed and worried him. He had his books and his teachers to instruct him on the real state of affairs and what had happened in the past that had eventually led to this best of all possible worlds.

In his early years he had been a loner, that is, so far as his fellow youngsters of the Technician caste were concerned. He had never been keen on spectator sports; watching others exercise for hours on end while he sat inactive, bored him. Nor did he, himself, particularly like to participate in kicking or throwing a ball about a field.

Happily for him, his father's home bordered on the Taos Pueblo National Monument, the sole remaining Indian reserve which preserved the way of life the Amerinds had enjoyed before the coming of the white man. Or, at least, it pretended to. Hundreds of thousands of gaping tourists came annually to observe the five-story-high adobe pueblo, to gawk at the kivas which they were not allowed to enter, to stare at the stoic face, blanket wearing, Taos tribesmen, with their long braided hair, as they had been stared at when Coronado's men first appeared on the scene, only twenty years after Cortes had stormed Mexico-Tenochtitlan and overthrew the Aztec power.

In actuality, most of the tribesmen had their homes in one of the two high-rise apartment buildings in the city of Taos, a few miles from the old pueblo. They commuted daily, changed their clothes to their pseudo-Indian trappings, and went into the Redman act, which included such items as keeping track of the small buffalo herd, ceremonial dances and pow-wows in the kivas. Rex Morris soon came to know that the Taos Indians were secretly in contempt of the whole show, but, of course, Rex was "in." His father was well known by the Taos tribesmen to have conquered the virus diseases and to be a medicine man beyond compare. He had been made an honorary member of the tribe. In spite of the fact that he had been awarded practically every international scientific honor available in his field, he had gone through the primitive ceremony with complete dignity.

So it was that Rex was free to ride the semi-wild Indian mustangs, to explore and hunt in the Twining Mountain area, to camp out in the Sangre de Cristos, to fish in streams usually barred to whites. It was a way of life largely disappeared in the Technate of North America.

And largely his companions were the Indian lads of the pueblo tribe of his own age, rather than the Technician caste boys in town. In actuality, the Indians had no standing in Technate society, in view of their status as wards of the government but it was fairly early in life that it was brought home to Rex Morris through teachers and youthful white contemporaries that *had* the Indians belonged, as did everybody else, they would undoubtedly have ranked in the effective caste. At most, a few might have made it to engineer status but certainly none among them, even the chiefs, would have been technicians.

Riding over the prairies behind the pueblo proper, Rex Morris couldn't have cared less as he thrilled to the pursuit of a jackrabbit, armed with primitive bow and arrow and egged on by the shrilling whoops of his half naked Indian friends.

But that was before he became fully aware of his father's unorthodoxy.

It was several years after he had eavesdropped on the argument with Mike Wheaton that the conversation came back to him. The situation was in many ways identical.

Three prominent scientists, all bearing the honorary

rank of Technician, had come from the East to consult his father. Rex had been introduced to them, had suffered the usual banalities directed at youth by adults, and had shortly retired to his den to study. He could have remained but obviously the talk was going to be completely over his head.

He had stretched out on his cot with a biography of Howard Scott, the pioneer Technocrat, but found it difficult to concentrate due to the hum of voices in the next room. Finally, he put the book down in disgust and opened the door a crack.

His father was holding forth in top form. "No. You have it all wrong, Fred. The original idea was good enough. Obviously, the most competent to run either an industry or a government should run them. A socio-economic system that doesn't provide for this is invalid. The mistake that the Technate has made has been not to perpetuate the rule of the most meritorious but the rule of a class. Theoretically, anyone born an effective can rise in rank even to the office of Supreme Technician but in actuality to jump a caste is all but impossible. The children of Technicians become the next generation's Technicians."

Professor Temple said huffily, "Like father, like son."

Rex Morris could picture his father shaking his head.

"No you're wrong, professor. Genetics doesn't work the way people wish it did. It isn't like father, like son. It's like father's ancestral statistics, like son's ancestral statistics, and it doesn't guarantee a damn thing about the individual. The genius can't guarantee his children will be extra bright and neither can he guarantee that the janitor's brats won't be the potential great achievers of the next generation. Take old Abraham Lincoln, descendant of a long line of nobodies. Genius himself, and the father of a line of descendants just like his ancestors—nobodies. No, genetics is a statistical roll-of-the-dice business."

Another voice broke in with, "If Lincoln hadn't married that dim wit Mary Todd, his children might have been of higher caliber."

And still another voice injected, "Alexander the Great

was the son of Philip of Macedonia, both military geniuses."

Leonard Morris said impatiently, "I'm not saying it's impossible, I'm just saying there's no guarantee. Napoleon was one of the greatest generals of all time, but his son, the Prince of Rome, was a scrawny little incompetent who couldn't have commanded a squad. Come now, gentlemen, the truth, how many great artists, writers, scientists, statesmen or whatever can you name whose children became equally prominent?"

"There are some," someone else said. "Dumas *père* and Dumas *fils,* the two French writers."

"Previous few," Leonard Morris insisted.

Professor Temple's voice came again. "See here, Leonard, are you attacking the government?"

"Of course I am. I would estimate that four out of five persons who hold down ranks of Senior Engineer and higher are incompetent. And the present situation is such that even those who are competent men are usually working in a field they know and care little about, their abilities wasted."

"These are dangerous sentiments, Morris," one of the other voices said with an element of heat.

"If we don't discuss them, who will?" Rex's father demanded.

"What do you offer as an alternative? For the first time in history, we have a society in which poverty has been eliminated. The people are happy. We no longer have the threat of war, or depressions or any of the other fears that formerly plagued us."

And Professor Temple, a sneer in his voice, said, "What would you do, turn the government over to the effectives, the dregs of society?"

There was a wry amusement in the older Morris' voice. "In a way, yes, I would. To the effectives and the engineers."

The other three laughed.

One said, "You're joking, of course."

"No, I'm not. We've got to get out of this rut. We've become static as a result of this fear of rocking the boat.

We don't *want* good men in decision making positions. They might take steps that would change things. We don't want innovations. The race is stagnating as a result. And a living life form can't stagnate, it either advances or it deteriorates, and so does a society."

One of the others snapped, "What's this got to do with the effectives and engineers taking over the government? That makes no sense at all, and besides that is outright subversive."

"I don't mean that the effectives should suddenly be elevated to the positions that Technicians hold today. I do think that our system of appointing personnel from the top down is wrong and that appointments should be from the bottom up."

"Nonsense," the professor snapped. "Nobody is more competent to appoint a man to a position than the official immediately above him."

"That's according to who is above him. If it's some clod who owes his job to the fact that a relative or friend is above *him*, then he's most likely incompetent to appoint his workers on the next lower level."

They fell silent for the moment, but it was an unhappy silence.

Leonard Morris pushed it. "The most capable to appoint a man to an office are those who work with him, his fellows. Nobody knows his abilities better than they. We need a return to the democratic principle, gentlemen."

Professor Temple snorted. "I refuse to listen to any more of this twattle, Morris. Let's get back to the field in which you are admittedly well based, bio-chemistry. Obviously, you know nothing of socio-economics."

In his den, young Rex softly closed the door again, and then stared at it, unseeingly. His face was worried.

It was about two weeks later, as Rex was returning from a ride with friends on the pueblo grounds that he spotted the official hover limousine parked before the Morris home. Coming closer, he scowled at the insigna on the side. You didn't see a good many official cars in the vicinity of Taos. The insigna was that of the Security Functional Sequence.

62

There was a chauffeur in the front seat, behind the manual controls. He yawned, obviously bored, and obviously waiting for someone inside. He was in the uniform of a Senior Effective but there was a stupid air about him that made Rex wonder how he had ever achieved even to that point.

Rex Morris made a sudden decision and rounded the corner of the house, rather than entering by the front door. He came to the window of his den and looked quickly up and down. There was nobody to be seen in any direction. Operating as quietly as possible, he slid open the window, looked up and down again, and then threw a leg over the sill. He emerged into his room beyond and quickly turned and closed the window behind him again.

The door to the living room was closed. He made his way to it, treading carefully, and pressed an ear against the paneling. He could make out only the hum of conversation, not words.

Very carefully, he opened the door a merest crack.

A cold, very official voice was saying, "Technician McCord died last month, leaving you the sole living man who carries the Hero Award. However, Leonard Morris, you are not untouchable. Have you ever heard of Erwin Rommel?"

His father's voice held puzzlement. "Marshal Rommel, the German general in the Second World War?"

"Field Marshal, and at the time of his death the second greatest hero of the German people."

"Who was the first?"

"Hitler. Frankly, I have often wondered what would have occured if the Fuehrer hadn't been engulfed by the Red hordes. Whether or not his Thousand Year Reich might not have evolved into a Technate."

Leonard Morris said dryly, "As I recall, friend Hitler was engulfed by more than the red hordes. There were other elements at the time that were not particularly fond of him."

"A great tragedy, perhaps. But at any rate, we were speaking of Field Marshal Rommel, the second most popular man in Germany. Despite that, when he made the mistake of opposing his commander he was given two alternatives. He could either commit suicide or stand trial and be hung. He was not untouchable. The German people were informed that he had died as a result of wounds taken in combat, after he had poisoned himself."

There was surprised shock in the older man's voice. "Are you threatening me, Technician?"

"Obviously. I am the Technician of the Security Functional Sequence of this area and have received various reports of your non-conformist, malcontent statements, made at random to anyone who will listen. This must end. I am warning you, Leonard Morris. Hero of the Technate or not, you will not make any subversive statements in this area."

Rex Morris could hear his father breathing heavily, but the older man for the nonce held his peace.

The police official wound it up. "Nor are you to leave Taos without checking with my office."

"You mean I'm under house arrest?"

"Call it that if you will. The news will not go out to the public media. It would cause too much of a stir if our sole living Hero of the Technate was revealed to be under surveillance."

On the following day, Rex Morris had approached his class adviser of the Educational Functional Sequence in Taos. The man, though of Technician background, bore only the rank of Junior Engineer and it was generally understood that he'd be lucky ever to get a better appointment. He simply didn't have the connections, even for the Educational Functional Sequence, to reach the higher rungs of the ladder. He usually bore a bitter air.

Rex Morris was not one of the students he saw most frequently, the boy doing practically all of his studies in his own home over the Tellscreen.

However, he assumed what he probably thought to be an intellectual, adult expression and said, "Well, Rex, if I may be so bold as to address the son of our most illustrious citizen by his first name . . . ?"

Great Scott, Rex thought inwardly, *some of that crud again.*

Aloud, he said, "Techno Blanding, it seems to me that it's about time I should join the Taos Young Technicians Patrol, the way you suggested a year or so ago."

His class adviser was somewhat taken aback. "You seemed rather definite in your refusal at that time."

"Well, yes sir. However, I've been studying up on the early fathers of the Technate, Howard Scott and all, and it seems to me that I'm getting to the age where I ought to, uh, begin to think in terms of putting my shoulder to the wheel. I've learned the Young Technician's Oath. You want me to recite it?"

"Well, no," the other said hurriedly. "It wouldn't be necessary. I've heard it so many times. But, I, ah, don't want to sound controversial, but I would have thought . . . well, your father. Are you sure that he is in favor of this?"

"Dad? Why, sure. He's always wanted me to join up with the other fellows in the patrol."

"He has? I gained the impression from some of the rumors around that he wasn't particularly enthusiastic about such organizations as the Young Technician's Patrol and the Technician's Junior Club. In fact, there was some hint about his home not being a suitable atmosphere for a young fellow such as yourself to be raised in."

"Gosh, the darndest rumors get around. Dad's all hot for me to join the patrol."

"Excellent, Rex! Then we'll expect you at the next patrol meeting."

That evening, at dinner, the older Morris was somewhat perplexed.

"The Young Technician's Patrol? It never occurred to me that you'd want to join that snobbish outfit, son." Leonard Morris, at this age, was already not a young man but his mental capacities were at their heighth and he spoke in a voice that indicated his vigor.

Rex said, uncomfortably, "Well, most of the Technician class boys belong, Dad. I don't like to be different.

65

"You don't? Why not?"

"Well, I guess I've been different enough already. It doesn't seem to get you very far."

"I see." There was a sad quality in his father's voice. "I won't stand in your way, of course. However, you realize that membership in this aristocratic outfit is going to conflict with your healthy activities with your Indian friends. What with your studies, you aren't going to have the time for both."

"Yeah, I suppose so. But that's the way it is. Sooner or later, you've got to think in terms of making your contacts, getting friends on your list that'll be able to give you a hand after you get out of school."

His father sighed.

By the end of six months, Rex Morris was Chief Technician of the Taos Young Technician's Patrol. When he reached the age of eighteen, he joined the Technician's Junior Club and by twenty was president of that young people's snob society.

9.

In his room, in his Uncle Bill's establishment, Rex Morris lay back on his couch, his hands behind his head and stared up at the ceiling. He was irritated by the position into which he had been thrust by Paula Klein having taken him to the speakeasy. Undoubtedly, that was the reason the Functional Sequence man had been following him. And, damn it, if there was one thing he didn't want it was to be trailed by an SFS man. Now his plans were of necessity changed, and he hadn't wanted to change them.

He let out a gust of air, and sat up. He adjusted his Beau Brummel revival cravat and called, "Tell-screen."

The screen was set in the wall on the opposite side of the room and was approximately a yard square. It lit up.

Rex Morris said, "I want the number of Techna Nadine Sims' residence, here in Greater Washington."

A robo voice said, "Carried out."

Rex Morris stolled over to the set and was standing before it when the striking face of Nadine Sims faded in. She was in a shimmery expensive looking something that did nothing whatsoever to detract from her charms. As at the Lizzy Mihms party, every hair was in place—for that matter, every pore.

She raised her eyebrows, smiled her quick smile. "Well, I'm taken aback. The earnest young man from the wooly West, seeking employment in the big city."

"All work and no play makes Jack a jerk, or however it goes," Rex grinned back at her. "How about living up to your promises?"

"Promises?" she said, frowning slightly. "As I recall I

was normally kinked before Lizzy Mihm's party finally dissolved. One usually gets at least normally kinked at one of Lizzy's parties. However, not so much so that I would have forgotten a promise. I am afraid, Techno Morris that you'll have to elucidate."

Rex said, pretending to be crestfallen, "You asked if I was in town for good and I replied that I was more interested in what it offered in the way of bad and thereupon you offered your services. And that's a promise in my book. And a promise made is a debt unpaid."

It came back to her and Nadine Sims trilled a laugh. "Guilty," she said. "And I always keep my promises. In that respect I am a good girl."

"Great. The only respect I hope. Would you be free this evening for fun and games?"

"Free as a bird."

"Hmmm," he said, as though considering that. "Let's not get controversial. Back home, I have four parakeets and they're all caged."

"Fool," she laughed. "About eight? We can have a couple of John Brown's Bodys while I give you a rundown on what the Entertainment Functional Sequence is offering these days in the way of fun and games as you call it, and then out on the town we can go."

"John Brown's Bodys?" Rex said. "That's a new one for me. What do John Brown's Bodys do to you?"

"In the morning," Nadine said, "you feel as though you're moldering in your grave. Eight, then?"

"I'll be there sharp."

Her face faded and he turned away from the screen and went toward the closet. He opened it and looked over his extensive wardrobe. Uncle Bill had insisted that he outfit himself elaborately. Evidently good grooming was of more importance in acquiring a suitable appointment than were brains.

He dressed carefully in the gray suit of an unassigned Techno in view of the fact that he wasn't certain where the evening might take him before it was through and one never knew when the prestige of his rank might be of value. The Beau Brummel cravat he kept on; they

68

seemed to be all the thing on the younger men about town.

Dressed, he paused thoughtfully over his luggage, came to a quick decision and ran a thumbnail along a long seam of a bag. The seam opened to reveal a small secret pocket inside. He selected several items from it and placed them strategically in various pockets of his clothes, making sure they didn't bulk. Then he pressed the seam back together and it knit tight. He returned the bag to the closet.

Rex Morris looked into the living room, but his uncle didn't seem to be about. Out on the town again, Rex decided. He didn't know how the old boy did it. For that matter, he didn't know how any of the Technician class, here in Greater Washington, stood the continual round of alcohol saturated parties.

He left the apartment and went through the usual routine of taking the elevator down to the 175th floor, where he could get an express to street level. And all over again he wondered what percentage of a person's time went into riding elevators in these high-rise apartments.

In front of the building, he dialed a single seater at the Transport FS box and stood at the curb whistling softly between his teeth as he waited. Evidently, it was more or less of a rush hour, since it took at least five minutes for his hover cab to arrive. He was in no great hurry.

The sun was setting, the city darkened except for here and there where lights already winked on. Rex Morris decided that sunsets were wasted on a city—any city.

The single seater whooshed up to the curb and the door automatically opened for him. Rex climbed in and said into the vehicle's tell-screen, "Coordinates unknown. Take me to the home of Techna Nadine Sims."

A voice said, "Carried out," and the small car slid into the street's traffic.

Rex leaned back and relaxed, watching the streets go by, the pedestrians, the fast moving idiocy of urban life. He had spent practically all of his years in the area once known as New Mexico. At least, comparatively, there was still room to breathe out there. However, there were other angles, and at this age of his, thirty, with education considered complete, a man had to take his stand, make his way, put in ten years of work before being eligible for retirement. He sighed. It wasn't a pleasant prospect, the immediate years before him.

The vehicle pulled up before a moderately large, ultramodern building, evidently one of the most recently constructed. It overlooked the Potomac river.

The tell-screen said, "Techna Nadine Sims resides in Terrace Apartment 3-B on the 63rd floor. Carried out."

Rex Morris stepped to the curb, looked up at the building and made a silent appreciative whistle. The residence was as swank as his uncle's building and Uncle Bill held Technician rank, even though retired.

There were a dozen elevators in the lobby but only one marked for his destination on the 63rd floor. He stepped inside and said, "Techno Rex Morris, calling on Techna Nadine Sims."

Evidently, she had already cleared him through the building's security, since the elevator tell-screen said, "Carried out," and Rex Morris began to whisk upward, slowly accelerating, reaching a peak of speed, then slowly decelerating.

Apartment 3-B was immediately across the way. He stood before the door screen and said, "Rex Morris. Right on schedule."

The door opened and as she was advancing upon him, sari-clad again although in more brilliant color this time. He suspected real silk. She had a very tall glass in each hand, one with contents half gone. She held the full one out to him.

"A John Brown's Body," she said. "No rest for the wicked. Whoever dreamed this one up didn't like sissies."

"Is it that bad? I thought the Rattlesnakes we drink back home were the end." He took the glass, silently toasted her, took a sip. He let his eyes go round and pretended to cough. "I just felt my arches fall," he said. "What in the world goes into this?"

She led the way back to the living room, obviously fully aware of his eyes taking in her figure. The room had

70

a tremendous view out over the river and one whole wall was transparent.

"Absinthe, slivovitz and a tiny bit of kirsch," she told him. "For best results, you let it blend together for at least a week."

He snorted, "By that time I would think that it would have bubbled itself away in chemical reaction. Either that or have eaten its way through the glass."

She found a couch, settled herself down on it and looked up at him over her glass. "And how goes the search for employment? Have you found an assignment as yet?" she asked, and then added mischievously, "Or have you been spending all of your time in the speak-easies?"

He stared at her. "How in the world did you know about that?"

Nadine Sims laughed. "There's a particularly viperish society commentator that I simply can't resist listening to of an afternoon. They seem to get bolder every week. You have to be in on all the latest to properly understand all his innuendoes but he managed to put over the idea that the son of Leonard Morris was evidently following in his father's footsteps."

Rex set down his glass with a bang of disgust. "Great Scott," he complained. "The old boy's habit of sounding off is going to haunt me the rest of my life. Why couldn't I have been born with the usual, normal parents?"

Nadine Sims was mildly amused. "I take it you don't approve of your father's, shall we say, unconventional beliefs."

He growled his continued disgust. "So far as I'm concerned he can think what he wants but I wish he'd keep it to himself." He took up his drink again and finished off half its contents, in one long pull. "I've had to put up with discrimination all my life. All I've ever wanted to do was have a good time, like everybody else. But what do I get? Ha! I meet what seems to be a perfectly ordinary girl and in fifteen minutes she's taken me to a speakeasy. Why? Because I'm Leonard Morris' son."

Nadine laughed at him. "Well, doesn't it have its advantages too? There must be something in being the son of the only living Hero of the Technate. The right schools. The right contacts. Hmmm, something has just occurred to me."

She came to her feet and went over to the autobar where she dialed two more of their drinks. She brought them back to him, this time settling down on the couch next to where he sat.

He said, "What just occurred to you? To get another drink? That occurs to me all the time."

"Silly," she said. "No, what I was thinking was that between the fact that your father is a Hero of the Technate and your uncle a retired Technician, we could probably take in the Flop House or the Techno-Casino."

"Sounds wonderful. I think I heard someone mention the Flop House but don't believe I've ever been there, though Great Scott knows, it seems to me that Uncle Bill has dragged me into every nightspot in town."

She said, "Oh, the Flop House is quite the place. No one under the rank of Senior Engineer, and not many of them. Real meat, you know. Even game from the preserves. Heavenly."

"Just so it isn't a speakeasy," Rex said. He checked his watch, then moved closer to her. He dipped a hand into his right pocket inconspicuously, then put his arm over her shoulders.

Her eyebrows went up and she looked at him quizzically but didn't move. "Not to change the subject over-abruptly," he said, his voice a murmur, "but how many people have told you that you look like Queen Nefretiti?"

"Nefretiti?" she said.

"Her bust is currently in the Louvre in the Common Europe Technate," he told her. "Egyptian. The most beautiful woman the world has ever seen." With the fingers of the hand he had dipped into his pocket, he stroked the lobe of her right ear.

Nadine Sims shivered. "Every day I learn something," she said. "Now I know who Queen Nefretiti was. Is this the way they operate in the West? Why do you think I look like this Nefretiti woman?"

72

He said, with mock criticism, "I suppose it's the neck and the line of the jaw. Ummm. Undoubtedly that's it. You have the same jaw, and the same perfect ears."

"And that's what a thirty year old . . ."

Her eyes glazed and she froze in position, her mouth half open, her glass held rigidly in her right hand.

10.

Rex Morris came to his feet. He quickly brushed a residue of brownish powder from the callused fingertips of his right hand, then looked down at her, his eyes narrow.

He passed a hand over her face without result, she remained motionless. He put a hand over her left breast but could not even detect her heart beat. With the tip of an index finger, he touched one of her eyeballs. No flicker of response.

Without further hesitation, he started for the back areas of her apartment, darting a quick glance at his wrist watch as he went. He found the kitchen, left by its back door. This was a crucial point now. Unless the service elevator was manually operated, the whole thing was off. He couldn't afford to have the fact that he had used the service elevator go into the building's computer banks.

It was manually operated. He took it all the way down to the cellars. There was no one there.

Rather than dial a hover car from this point, he walked up the ramp on his toes, silently. The alley was dark before him, but he hesitated before leaving the entranceway to the apartment building. From an inner pocket, he brought forth a pair of what seemed sun glasses, donned them and then from another pocket brought forth a gadget no larger than a packet of cigarettes.

He played the infra-red flashlight about the service alleyway which ran between the towers of the high-rise building and caught a figure lounging in a doorway across from him. Rex Morris sucked in his breath. He hadn't figured on being followed this evening. Certainly not to the point where there would be a man stationed both before and behind the building.

He withdrew further into the shadows and brought a small hand weapon from a hip pocket. He knelt, took as rock-like a position as he could, using both hands to steady his aim, and pressed the trigger, once, twice. The weapon hissed and across the alleyway the other folded up, crumpled to his knees and then went prone.

Rex Morris slipped the gun into the side pocket of his jacket and sped across to the Security agent. He manhandled the SFS man back into the doorway in which he had been standing, propped him in such wise as to appear as though he had passed out from drink, on the off chance that someone else might come by and spot the fellow. Still hurrying he then made his way down the alley and to the street, merging in the pedestrian traffic there.

He walked a full block before summoning a hover car, and then rode it to within two blocks of his destination, using the manual controls. He dismissed the cab at that point and strode rapidly the rest of the way. As he entered the old building there, he darted another look at his watch and said a silent prayer to unknown gods that everything was going on schedule.

There was no elevator in this building that went back to an older era. He took the stairway to the third floor and used a key there to let himself into a small efficiency apartment. No one was present. In fact, the apartment had an appearance of long disuse.

He went to the sole window that let upon the main street and manually opened it. He wanted no possible record of his voice on the robo-command. He looked out without getting near enough that anyone below could have identified him, even had they been looking.

Down the street approximately 300 yards, a large limousine was drawing up before an official building.

He shot another look at this watch, hurried to a corner

and from a bag of golf clubs drew a sporting rifle, complete with telescopic sights. As he moved back to the window, he threw the bolt, checking the shell before ramming it home into the breech. High velocity, armor piercing.

At the window, he sat on a foot stool, bracing one elbow on a knee, rested the rifle barrel on the window ledge. And waited.

The limousine was disgorging its passengers.

The man for whom he was waiting stepped forth and hesitated momentarily while shaking hands with another of the car's occupants. He then stepped back and turned preparatory to entering the building.

He was fully in the crosshairs of the scope.

Rex Morris breathed deeply, then held his breath and squeezed. The silenced gun coughed and a spurt of dust exploded on the granite wall behind the target. The man's head came up abruptly and looked around in quick alarm.

Rex Morris muttered, shot the bolt again, and tried for another shot.

His target was now darting for the building entrance. A dozen security men, who suddenly materialized from seemingly nowhere, weapons in hand, were on the move. Five or six of them crowded around their superior.

The second shot blasted into the metal door several inches higher than the heads of the running men. All ducked even as they passed through to security beyond.

Rex Morris grunted, dropped the rifle and hurried for the apartment door. He sped down the stairs to the street, and slowed to a stroll as he issued forth from the building. He figured that it would take them anywhere from fifteen minutes to half an hour to find the window from which the shot had come. Meanwhile, Rex blended into the pedestrian traffic.

He walked two blocks. At one point he broke the lenses of his infra-red glasses before dropping them surreptitiously into a street waste receptacle. Further on he tossed his flashlight into the rubble of a construction job, when no one was around. He stripped his gloves from his

76

hands and left them, with his dart gun, in another receptacle further on.

He checked his timepiece, then dialed a hover car at a corner Transport FS box, and, once more using manual controls, returned to the vicinity of Nadine Sims apartment house. He hustled down the alley, checking the Security agent and found him still under the effect of the two darts Rex Morris had used on him earlier.

He returned to the service elevator and took it to the floor below the one on which Nadine Sims had her apartment, and from there ascended the stairs. In moments, he was back in the Sims kitchen.

He took two full minutes to run cold water over his wrists, to wash his face, to brush his clothes and to catch his wind. Then he returned to the couch at which she sat, still staring straight ahead. He ran a hand before her eyes again without any response whatsoever.

Rex sat down next to her in exactly the position he had before and looked at his watch for a last time. He took up his glass from the cocktail table where he'd set it earlier and held it at half mast, looking into her face.

Within five minutes her eyes cleared and she said, as though she had never been interrupted, ". . . bachelor particularly notices in a woman these days?"

Rex shrugged and took a pull at his drink. "That's me. I'm a neck man. Figures are all very nice, perhaps, but all women have pleasant figures these days, at least all Techno women do. But necks . . . ! he took a deep breath and let a mock swooning expression run over his face.

"You fool," she said.

"About this evening," Rex changed the subject. "What happens after the Flop House?"

She pursed her lips. "Let's see. What does the Entertainment FS have on a Techno level these days? I suppose you have no interest in slumming among the effectives."

"You're the guide," he told her. "However, it's been my experience that the effectives are a bit on the drab side. Their entertainment inclined to be grim."

She looked at the dainty bejeweled watch on her wrist. "It's later than I thought. Let's hurry along and we can discuss the balance of the evening at the Flop House. Actually, I understand one never knows what will develop there. You'll usually run into some sort of party that spontaneously erupts. And that can lead to anything."

Rex grunted skeptically. "Well, don't introduce me by name. My name has a way of chilling the air. Or, at least my father's does, and it always winds up rubbing off on me."

She looked at him, her face quizzical "You really have a case of anti-daditis, don't you?" She took a sip of her drink and then began to stand. She frowned down into the glass. "Seems to have got awfully warm in such a short time. The ice is completely melted.

Rex finished his own drink in one long gulp. "Mine's all right," he said. "Let's get along."

"I'll go get my coat," she said, still frowning vaguely at her warmish drink.

11.

At the entrance to the Flop House, which was on the ground floor of a high-rise in one of the best parts of town, Rex Morris was impressed. A uniformed attendant opened the door of their car, murmured a polite good evening, turned and preceded them to the door of the restaurant which he manually opened.

Immediately inside, as they gave up Nadine's light coat to a bright young thing garbed in a minus-skirt, Rex said to his companion, "How swank can you get? I didn't know there were still any members of the Service Functional Sequence. I thought they had folded that up years ago."

Nadine Sims said, "If I'm not wrong, the servants you find here are all members of the Security Functional Sequence."

"Oh?" He looked surprised. "I'd think even an effective would consider it beneath him."

"These are hardly effectives," Nadine said dryly. "And the principle job is—so I understand—not just opening doors, taking coats and hats, or ushering diners to their tables. But isn't the subject becoming, somewhat . . . say, sticky?"

Rex Morris immediately switched to some banality about the decor, which in actuality seemed on the overdone side to him. But then, he was used to the simplicity of Taos.

An unctous faced type approached them, his voice dripping with condescension. "I am sorry, but I am afraid this establishment is restricted to . . ."

Nadine Sims said with hauteur. "You are making a mistake, my man. This is Techno . . ."

The other was shaking his head, sadly, "Techno rank is insufficient, I am afraid. The Flop House is reserved for . . ."

Nadine overrode him. ". . . Rex Morris, the son of Hero of the Technate Leonard Morris."

The other was already reversing his engines. "Of course, how stupid of me, Techno Morris. Your uncle is with us tonight, will you be at his table?"

Nadine said "If I know your uncle, Rex, we'd both be kinked before we ever got out of here, and we did want to make a night of it, didn't we?"

"Right as rainbows," Rex said, and to the head waiter, "A table of our own, if you please."

They were given a table pleasantly located near the dance floor.

"Heavens to Veblen," Nadine whispered to him. "You'll have to admit that your father's name has its advantages when it comes to impressing flunkies and opening doors."

"I suppose so," he said, as though bored.

Rex Morris looked about the room. At the far side of the dance floor his uncle Bill was waving to him jovially. The older Morris was seated at a table with half a dozen others, three or four of whom Rex recognized as of Technician rank, including Marrison, the textile bigwig. They all seemed to be well into their cups.

Nadine Sims had adjusted her sari to her satisfaction, had ordered a Double Weeping Willow from the waiter who had scurried up to their table, and now let her eyes rove the room, undoubtedly, woman-like, to check out what others were wearing. She smiled at half a dozen different parties, nodded here and there. On the face of it, our Nadine enjoyed her luxury, and this establishment

80

must have been one of the most luxurient in Greater Washington, and hence in the world.

She said dryly, "You don't seem overpopular with Techna Paula Klein tonight."

"I beg your pardon?"

She said, "Paula Klein, sitting over there with Technician Matt Edgeworth. Didn't I detect a malicious glare?"

Rex Morris sought Paula out, but now she was talking in animation with the hefty SFS Technician seated across from her. The police official, somehow, seemed out of his element in the ultra-swank Techno class restaurant. Of all present, he alone was unpossessed of the aristocratic aura which evolves with long generations of the manor born. His face was on the rugged side, his hair even just slightly unkempt, his gestures not so suave as his fellow Technicians and Prime Technicians at the neighboring tables.

Rex Morris let his upper lip curl, portraying disgust. "Whom did you say that effective dressed in Technician clothes was?"

Nadine Sims eyes narrowed infinitesimally. She said, her voice even, "That's Matt Edgeworth. Don't you remember? You must have met him at Lizzy Mihm's party. In a way, you're right. He worked his way up. Quite a career." She added, idly, "And I understand it possibly hasn't reached its peak. Warren Klein, you know, the Prime Technician of the Security Functional Sequence, is past retirement age, and rumored ill besides."

Rex Morris snorted deprecation. "No effective could ever become a member of the Congress of Prime Technicians. Even if he was appointed by the other FS heads, certainly the Supreme Technician would veto such a farce."

The drinks had arrived and Nadine Sims stirred hers idly with a swizzle stick. "There's nothing in law or tradition against it," she said. "And promotion in the Security Functional Sequence is considerably easier than in some others. The requirements are different, of course. Not everybody has the qualities needed in top police officials."

Rex snorted his contempt. "Can you name a single

case in the past century, of an effective born getting to the Congress of Prime Technicians?"

"He's already reached Technician rank," she said. "Only one step to go."

Rex gave a disgusted shrug of his aristocratic shoulders, and didn't bother to answer her.

She said softly, "I understand he doesn't think so highly of you, either."

"What in the name of the Great Scott do you mean by that?" His attention was regained.

She put down her swizzle stick, lifted the glass to her lips and watched his face. "The gossip grapevine has it that he wouldn't mind at all a slip on your part, one that would allow him to have you into a Technocourt."

Rex Morris was aghast. "Great Scott, why? I've hardly met the lout."

"You seem to be rather emphatic about a man you've had no contact with," she said. "How do you know you wouldn't find him reeking with compatibility if you did meet?"

He glared across the room at the Security Technician. "It seems unlikely."

"Is it because he's with the beautiful and charming Paula Klein?" she asked.

"Certainly not. Besides, it's as you said. I'm evidently on Techna Klein's unacceptable list."

She finished her drink and tapped on the side of the slender stemmed glass with her swizzle stick. The waiter smoothed to the table with two more of the same.

Nadine said idly, "You'd think that in a city of this size there'd be scads of eligible young men, but it evidently isn't that simple for a girl of Paula's rank."

He scowled his incomprehension at her, looking the highly spoiled hereditary aristocrat that he was.

She said, "Paula's brother and father were both Prime Technicians. But most of all, the Supreme Technician is her cousin. Now, really, you can't get much higher than that, can you?"

"Cousin of the Supreme Technician?" Rex repeated. "I didn't know that."

Nadine swizzled her new drink. "Not many eligible young men in that rarified altitude. Of course, the son of a Hero of the Technate . . ."

Rex grunted his disgust at that idea. "My father's notoriety outweighs that prestige."

"I doubt it. When you get to Paula's height anything can be forgiven. For that matter, one of her grandfathers opposed the Temple. How much further can you non-conform?"

Rex Morris said impatiently, "What's all this got to do with that oaf over there being out to get me?"

Nadine Sims smiled at him charmingly. "As you pointed out, it's been more than a century since anyone born an effective reached the Congress of Prime Technicians. It wouldn't hurt anyone with such ambitions to marry himself to Paula Klein."

Rex pursed his lips and whistled silently. "Oh, oh," he said. "I suppose I'd better let it be known around that I'm not interested in the young lady's charms. Otherwise, I'll wind up having him arresting me for subversive conversation every time I open my mouth to yawn."

"Then you're *not* bewitched by Techna Klein?" Nadine said.

He reached a hand across the table to pat hers. "My dear Nefretiti the Second," he told her. "Remember? I'm a neck man. And if you'll just compare hers and yours . . ."

She laughed lightly, but darted a glance across the room at Paula. "Actually, she seems not at all unattractive in a rather . . . well, earnest sort of way."

"Now that's what I call damning by faint praise," Rex grinned at her.

There was a slight commotion near the entrance and after a moment Technician Matt Edgeworth came hurriedly to his feet, forgetting to excuse himself to Paula Klein, and hurried his way toward the distraction, swiveling his hips like a broken field football runner as he progressed between the tables. The big man could move fast enough when he had the occasion.

There seemed to be an animated discussion at the far

83

end of the room which finally could be hardly ignored by anyone present in the establishment.

Eventually, Matt Edgeworth made his way back through the tables again and to the center of the dance floor. He held his hands up above his head for attention, his face an emotionless mask.

Rex said to Nadine Sims," What in the devil is going on? What does the big clown want?"

She said, scowling perplexity, "I wouldn't know. Evidently something important has happened."

Matt Edgeworth was saying, "May I have everyone's attention, please." He paused, waiting for the buzz of surprised comment to fade away. "A matter of greatest importance and since such a large percentage of the city's ranking officials are present . . . You are all familiar with the Prime Technician of the Security FS, Warren Klein . . ."

A man approximately ten years Edgeworth's senior had followed him to the dance floor's edge and now stepped to the middle of the stage, while his subordinate retreated several paces.

Rex Morris could recognize family similarities to Paula Klein's in the newcomer's face. Warren Klein wore a gray suit, a gray greatcoat over his shoulders like a cloak in traditional Prime Technician style. He was a handsome man, but there was a wanness about his face that indicated poor health.

He looked about the crowded room, his expression drawn. "Possibly an hour ago I was the subject of an assassination attempt as I left my car to enter my offices."

He waited until the uproar that greeted his words had faded away. It took several minutes.

He held up a hand for quiet. "The only such attempt on a member of the Congress of Prime Technicians in modern memory. My first reaction was that it was the work of a single crackpot, possibly with a personal grudge. However . . ."

He drew an envelope from an inner pocket. ". . . one of my aides has brought this to my attention. It arrived in last week's post and was not sooner revealed to me since it seemed nothing more than the raving of a mental case. Such are not unknown in our office. However, after to-night's events."

He read the letter aloud. "Prime Technician Warren Klein: You are incapable of holding the office to which you have been appointed. Consequently, unless your resignation is announced in the immediate future, your life is forfeit. The race stagnates as a result of the usurpation of position by incompetents."

Warren Klein looked up and swept the Flop House with his eyes, going from table to table. He said, "This letter is signed, *The Nihilists*."

Warren Klein held up his hand again to silence them after a buzz had gone through the room to swell into a minor uproar.

He said, "For those who are unacquainted with the term, nihilism was a 19th century revolutionary movement which stressed the need to destroy existing economic and social institutions to prepare for the establishment of a supposedly better order. Direct action such as assassinations and arson against the members of the then existing government were among the methods utilized by the nihilists. These terrorists were successful in killing some of the highest ranking officials of the day, including Tsar Alexander the Second of Russia. They sometimes blew up whole trains in their efforts to assassinate a single man. In brief, they were not to be underestimated, in spite of the fact that they were fanatics."

Some of the Flop House occupants were on their feet, their faces expressing emotion ranging from complete disbelief to hysterical shock. For the moment, their voices drowned out the Prime Technician of their Security Functional Sequence.

The volume of Warren Klein's voice rose. "Preliminary investigation indicates that tonight's assassination attempt was well and thoroughly organized. I escaped with my life by a small margin and due to the loyal efforts of my men. But this is not the most important point." He held a moment of silence, to emphasize what he was about to say.

"The point is that this morning the Supreme Technician himself received a similar letter, worded almost exactly the same as the one I have just read."

From across the room a voice gasped, "So did I! I . . . I thought it was nonsense." The speaker was Technician Marrison, now cold sober, frightened out of his cups.

"And I!" someone else shouted. "I got one too. It came in the mail only yesterday."

Prime Technician Warren Klein let his eyes go completely around the room again. "We must face reality. For the first time in generations the Technate is faced with a revolutionary movement. The Security Functional Sequence expects every member of the Techno caste to cooperate to the fullest. My men are alerting everyone of rank in the city. Further information and instructions will be released to you through your individual functional sequences.

"In case of further messages or anything else pertaining to the Nihilists that comes to your attention, please contact my assistant Technician Matt Edgeworth."

12.

The Security Prime Technician, visably tired after speaking to the room without benefit of loud speaker, broke off and turned back to Matt Edgeworth. Still standing, they spoke urgently to each other in voices too low to carry to where Rex Morris and Nadine Sims sat.

Nadine bit her under lip, and looked in their direction. She seemed to come to a conclusion and came to her feet, apologetically. She said to Rex, "I've just remembered an appointment. No don't get up. We'll just have to postpone this lovely evening for another time."

Rex had already come to his own feet, in spite of her protest, but she was gone—in the direction of the two Security bigwigs.

Rex grunted, "I'll bet you just remembered an appointment."

He took up his half empty glass and wandered in the direction of the table that had been occupied by his uncle and party. At the present, practically everyone in the room was on their feet. At least, all the men were. Here and there, about the Flop House, feminine members of the Technician caste remained seated, their faces in an expression of being put upon, usually, rather than in alarm.

Technician Marrison was blurting, ". . . shoot 'em

down. That's what I say. Round 'em up and shoot 'em down like dogs. That's what they are, rabid dogs!"

But Uncle Bill, who didn't seem to have got quite as far into his cups as most of them, said wryly, "We're going to have to catch them before that's very practical, Fred."

The textile technician spun on him, a bit wildly perhaps, in view of the mildness of the opinion stated. "I could expect some dissent from you, William Morris, in view of the known opinions of your brother."

"Good Howard," someone else blurted. "Are we going to start arguing among ourselves? Who knows, when we walk out of here, if some sniper will take a shot at us?"

"Right," somebody else said, semi-hysterically. "We either hang together, we of the Technician caste, or we'll hang separately. But Fred's right. We've got to show them no mercy. Order the Security Functional Sequence to shoot them down on sight."

Rex Morris was taking it all in from the sidelines. He looked over at his uncle.

And that worthy was still wryly disgusted, in spite of the reproof from Marrison. "How can we shoot them at sight, if we've never seen one of them?"

"You know what I mean," the other told him.

Rex decided that nothing of any relevance was going to be said in this gathering at this stage of the game. They were conducting themselves like a bunch of old women. He wandered off, looked about the room for Nadine Sims and couldn't spot her. He made his way to the entrada. The Flop House was emptying and the entry was crowded. Rex slipped through the chattering, shrilling Technician caste habitues of the place to the sidewalk beyond. There too were chattering, milling, excited groups, some arguing inanely, some waiting for their summoned cars.

Rex decided that with this large a crowd, it would take an age to summon a cab and so wandered off to the right and headed down the street hands nonchalantly in pockets.

He strode several blocks before concluding that the

chances were remote that he was being followed. If he had been tailed to the Flop House, he had undoubtedly lost his man in the excitement. He decided to walk on back to his uncle's apartment building. The air would do him good and he wanted the chance to think things out a bit. All the bets were down now, there was no turning back.

Deep in his thoughts, he rounded a corner and ran full tilt into another pedestrian. She dropped her bag, almost fell, before he caught her with both hands.

"Look where you're . . ." she began, then pulled it short when she took in his gray Techno caste suit.

"I'm awfully sorry," he said. "Terribly clumsy of me."

"Oh, no. That's all right . . . sir." She added hurriedly, "It was my fault."

They both bent to pick up her purse and banged heads.

They straightened and Rex said, "Great Scott, we're going to kill each other before the night's out." He held up a hand as though to restrain her. "Now, let me do it this time."

He bent and picked up her bag and held it out. She was attired in the dress of a Junior Engineer of the Statistic Functional Sequence, in short, she had an assignment in the National Data Banks of, this, the computerized society. She must have been approximately Rex's own age or wouldn't have had an assignment, but she looked no more than twenty-five and projected a bright, perky quality. She was highly likeable on first sight.

She said, "Thank you . . . sir."

Rex said, "Sir, indeed. You make me feel like an old man. Besides, I gave you a good bang and you should be hating my guts." He looked at her speculatively. "I'm not trying to be fresh, but let me buy you a drink."

Suddenly she chuckled. "Fresh?" she said. "Now I bet you had to practice that one. The only time I've ever heard that term was on historical Tri-Di romances. You're not from Greater Washington. What part of the country do you hail from, stranger."

"Oh, oh," Rex groaned. "Don't tell me I've got that heavy a Western accent? It's a secret but it's true I'm new

89

in town. I've been out wandering around trying to get the feel of the place. And how about that drink?"

She frowned slightly and looked at his Techno gray suit again. "There's a lot of restrictions in this neighborhood. I doubt if they'd let me into a Techno bar. Senior Engineers, yes. but I'm only a Junior."

"Well, let's go to an engineer caste place, then. I'm building up a thirst by the minute."

"You wouldn't mind?"

"Why should I?" He took her arm and they turned to return in the direction from which she had just come.

She looked up at him from the side of her eyes. "My name's Adele," she said.

"Fine, Adele, I'm Rex."

The place she was leading them to was only half a block down the street, and on the street level. It was almost a hundred percent automated, but an Entertainment Functional Sequence receptionist met them at the door. His eyebrows went up when he saw Rex Morris' garb.

"Ah, sir," he began, "this is . . ."

"I know what it is. Do I look like an idiot?" Rex clipped. "Please see us to a table."

The other flushed. "Yes sir. Of course. I mean . . . no, sir. This way please."

A few more eyebrows went up as they progressed through the tables to a favorable one set in an attractive niche. However, if a Techno wanted to go slumming there was certainly no reason why he shouldn't. Senior and Junior Engineers certainly took in effective caste entertainments when they felt like it.

Seated, Rex looked about the place in approval. It seated several hundred and was quite packed. It boasted far from the swank of the Flop House, but there was a comfortable something in the air that the lavish Technician caste establishment hadn't had. You drank a drink in this place, instead of sipping it, Rex decided.

The girl looked Rex Morris over more carefully and evidently approved of what she saw. So did Rex for that matter. She was a cute little bit.

He looked down at the menu, set in the auto-table top. "What'll it be?" he asked her.

"You're the boss."

"I've been drinking Weeping Willows," Rex said, "but I don't see them listed here."

She said dryly, "If I'm not mistaken they're based on French champagne. A bit on the exotic side for an engineer."

He looked at her in surprise. "Oh? I didn't know that. I thought you could get anything in an engineer caste establishment that you can anywhere else."

She said, no rancor in her voice, "Well, you can't. Such expensive imports are limited to Technician rank places. It all has to do with balance of trade with the Common Europe Technate. As I understand it, theoretically a Technate is self-sufficient but there are some items, such as luxuries produced only in certain world areas, that have to be imported. To import, you must export, to balance it all out, and there are precious few items these days that we produce that Common Europe has any need for."

He had to laugh. "You obviously *are* from Statistics. Well, you suggest it."

"How about Tequila Coolers?"

Rex Morris didn't particularly like the fiery Mexican spirit but he dialed two, after putting his Universal Credit Card in the payment slot.

While they waited for the auto-table to deliver the drinks, she said, her head cocked slightly to one side, "You know, I think this is the first time I've ever had a drink with a Techno."

"Oh, we're not so formal out in Taos. I imagine that the Technate's capital is a little more straitlaced than our boondocks."

The center of the table sank and returned immediately with two long, cold drinks. They took them up and made a gesture of a toast.

"Of course, I'm not criticising the way things are handled here," he added.

"Of course not," she said automatically, and then her

eyes widened. She said in a hushed voice, "Rex. And you're new in town and from Taos. Why you must be . . ."

He looked at her in silence.

She darted a look at her watch. "Good Howard, I've forgotten. I'll have to get along."

"Sure?" he asked, not attempting to disguise his disappointment.

"I'm afraid so." She took a quick sip of her all but untouched drink and came to her feet.

Rex shrugged and stood as well and followed her toward the door.

Outside, on the street, he began to put his hand out for a goodbye shake, but she said, "Look, Rex Morris, if you still want that drink we can have it up at my place."

He scowled down at her. "What goes on here?"

"That place is bugged."

"Bugged?"

"Electronic mini-mikes at each table. All conversations are monitored by the computers."

"Great Scott, *why?*"

"Who am I to question the government?" She said humorously.

"But, what difference does it make? Why should they bother?"

She looked at him strangely. "You're the son of Leonard Morris and you ask that?"

"Of course."

"I heard on a news broadcast that you were in town and the innuendo was that you had already begun to frequent speakeasies."

"I was taken to one inadvertently," Rex said.

She gave a short disbelieving laugh. "You don't have to alibi to me. I've been in one or two myself. At any rate, as soon as I realized who you were, in there I thought we'd better get out. Already what you had said about things being straitlaced here in Greater Washington bordered on the controversial, a little on the critical side. I thought we'd better get out before the monitor began checking us more carefully."

92

He fell in step beside her and they proceeded down the street on foot.

He said, as though mystified, "I didn't know things had gone that far. How do you happen to know about it?"

"I work in the department involved. "I'm a Junior Engineer in charge of several banks of monitors."

"But, Great Scott, such an undertaking would involve literally thousands, tens of thousands of people. You'd have to have half the working force of the town monitoring each other."

She shook her head. "No. It's done with computers. They're set to check every conversation. If certain key words come up that indicate that certain controversial subjects are being discussed, they tape it in its entirety and refer it to one of us Junior Engineers." She added, sourly, "You'd be surprised how many conversations I have to play back to check, and how boring most conversations can be."

"Well, what happens if you tune in on somebody talking about changing the government or something really far out, like that?"

She grimaced. "Isn't that obvious. We notify Security and they take over from there on in."

Rex Morris blurted, "Heavens to Veblen!"

She cocked her head again in the perky mannerism she had and said, mockingly, "Why, Techno Morris, you aren't expressing criticism of the way the government conducts itself?"

"No, of course not," he said hurriedly. "I was simply surprised at the institution."

"Here we are," she said coming up on an apartment building which, though enormous, had not quite the swank of those that housed William Morris, Lizzy Mihm and Nadine Sims. It was, undoubtedly, largely devoted to engineer caste inhabitants although Rex knew that often, even in these building, Technos would take over the more desirable quarters such as the penthouses and terrace apartments on the top floors. There was status in having your apartment as high as possible. Often, even in the most swank high-rise apartment buildings, there would be

93

effectives living in smaller quarters on the lower levels and in the basements.

He followed her inside and to the elevator banks, noting that it had been unnecessary to identify himself with his Universal Credit Card to gain admission. Evidently, security wasn't deemed quite so necessary in establishments devoted largely to engineers, as it was where Technicians predominated.

She had her moderately sized apartment on the 18th floor and when they appeared the identity screen recognized her and the door opened before them.

She led the way into the living room, tossed her purse to a table, gestured sweepingly and said, "Behold my castle. Make yourself to home, stranger. I'll dial that interrupted Tequila Cooler." She went over to an autobar which sat in one corner.

Actually, Rex didn't truly want the drink, but he did desire to talk with her a bit more. His contacts, here in Greater Washington, had been almost exclusively with those of Technician rank and he was curious. Besides that, the girl had an intriguing charm, and Rex Morris was far from immune to feminine charm.

He took a chair and crossed his legs and looked about him. The apartment was pleasant enough and obviously its occupant had a flair for decoration, a sense of taste. It came to him that he had been in many a Techno establishment that didn't show nearly as much, in spite of considerably more room, and added resources. Ostentacious living was the theme of Techno life, and he wondered fleetingly if those of engineer status actually lived on higher level, despite supposedly being of lower caste.

She brought their drinks, gave him one and then sat down opposite on a couch, adjusting her minus-skirt. She raised her glass in toast. "Well, all over again, cheers, Rex Morris."

He responded, then said, "All right, you know my full name and something about me, though evidently nothing to the good. Now tell me about you."

She made a move and shrugged slightly. "Not much to tell. Very average young woman. Adele Briarton. Thirty-

94

one years of age, and feeling every minute of it. Orphan Finished school at M.I.T. Top honors, spare my blushes Specialized in computer technology. On graduation wa: grabbed up real quick by Statistics Functional Sequence Given an assignment right here in the date banks in tha section affiliated with Security—not necessarily my own choice. Junior Engineer. Very smart girl. I.Q. of 142."

"Well," Rex said, impressed. "With all that in the way of background, you must really be on your way up Someday I'll be reading about Adele Briarton making Technician."

She looked at him strangely. "To the contrary, I'm already as high up as I'll ever get. I'm lucky to be this high You usually start, even with my training, as a Senior Effective, at most."

"I.Q. of 142, top honors from MIT? That's the best technical school in the Technate, isn't it?"

She said, a faint edge of bitterness in her voice, "Yes, it is. By far. Where did you study, Techno Morris?"

"Rex," he said easily, assuming his characteristic languid air. "Oh, around. I didn't really specialize in anything. Or, rather, in too many things. I'd lose interest in whatever and switch schools, or at least subjects." He snorted self-deprecation. "I was my father's despair. I don't know how I ever got through my education."

"I see. I would think that as your father's son you would have gone into the sciences."

"Oh, no. I'm not the studious type, not ambitious, and have no desire to follow in my father's footsteps." He switched back to her. "But what's that got to do with you not going any further? Don't you like your job, Adele?"

"I love it. I spent the last ten years of my studies working in computers. You're the reason."

He had been about to take another sip of his drink, but he took his glass away from his mouth. "I beg your pardon?"

"I said, you're the reason why I'll never get higher in rank than a Junior Engineer. Or, at least, it's very unlikely. I might, at most, make Senior Engineer, before retirement."

"Oh, come now. How could I in any way be responsible? We'd never even met before we crashed into each other down there on the street." He was truly puzzled by her.

She gave a little snort. "Oh, maybe not you as an individual. But you came here to Greater Washington for an assignment, didn't you? I'll bet your I.D. rates you at least as a Two category, possibly even a One." She gave him a quick impish grin, though there was a wry quality there too. "I understand all this from the gossip broadcast I heard."

"Well, yes, for an assignment, but, well, I still don't know what you're talking about."

She sighed and set her glass down. "If somebody offered you a job as Senior Engineer in the Statistics Functional Sequence, which is one of the largest in Greater Washington, would you take it?"

"Why . . . I suppose so. I really have no preference."

"What do you know about computers, data banks, records, statistics, electronics, and so forth and so on?"

"Why, I don't know. I'd have to take a certain amount of training for the job." He was uncomfortable.

"She shook her head. "No, not really. Or, at least, not much and very superficial. You'd spend most of your time having cocktails before lunch, with your fellow Technos, and a few quick ones, between lunch and knock-off time, and then do your wheeler-dealering over nightclub tables in the evenings. But remember I told you I had spent ten years studying in the field?" She added wryly, "At MIT, with an I.Q. of 142. I won't ask you what your I.Q. is Techno Morris."

He remained quiet.

She said, "If your Technician uncle—his hame is William Morris, isn't it? I understand he's quite a playboy around town. At any rate, if he twists the arm of the Technician in charge of my Functional Sequence, or, even more, the arm of the Prime Technician, possibly for former favors done, it is quite possible that you could land the job immediately above me. Then you'd be my Senior Engineer. After possibly five years at that position,

96

once again, if you have pull enough, and I suppose you do have you'll possibly be made Technician when your uncle's buddy retires. And in another five years, particularly if your father comes to heel a bit and resumes his former close position with the Congress of Prime Technicians and the Supreme Technician, you might even be jumped to Prime Technician of the Statistics Functional Sequence. Let us carry it further. When the Supreme Technician dies, or voluntarily retires, you might be elected to that office. But, Rex Morris, you still wouldn't know how to throw a switch on the simplest computer that I supervise."

"I detect a bit of bitterness," Rex said quietly, taking another sip of the drink that he didn't really want.

She shook her head wearily. "No. Not really, I suppose. It's just the way things are. Didn't they used to have some sort of saying, you can't fight City Hall? In actuality, not one person out of three under the Technate really is required. And it applies on both ends of the working force."

"Aren't you getting a bit controversial, Miss Briarton?" Rex Morris felt it was about time to get around to something like that.

"When I'm speaking to the son of Leonard Morris?"

He didn't answer that. He wanted to hear what she had to say. He'd never really sounded out anyone of engineer caste to this extent before and was intrigued.

She said, "Most effectives are redundant. Long past, the common laborer became a drug on the labor market. Automation took over his job. But an idle man is potentially a dangerous man, so under the Technocate we give them make-work jobs. Some are necessary, of course, and always will be, no matter what the degree of automation, but largely they are redundant. They do very little, this largest element in our industrial system, that couldn't be done, and undoubtedly better, by a Junior Effective or a Senior one equipped with the latest in technological innovations."

"You said both ends of the working force."

"Yes, of course. The technician caste is as largely redundant as the effective. They no longer fill a need. Just as the feudalistic class and the capitalistic class later became redundant, so now have the Technicians."

"But who would make the ultimate plans, if there was no Congress of Prime Technicians, and the Technicians who carry out their orders?"

She sighed. "I assume the same ones who do it now. Their supposed assistants. Their staffs. Some Senior Engineers, but largely Junior Engineers and Senior Effectives, working, of course, with computers and the latest technology. You don't truly fool yourself into believing that you hereditary Technicians really do any work do you, Techno Morris? You don't you know."

He said quietly, "I got the impression that you were an admirer of my father. Do you contend that he didn't work? He is, of course, retired now."

She shrugged. "There are exceptions. Some are very notable ones. But they are exceptions. The Technician caste, as a *class* is parisitical."

"So what would you do about it, Adele?"

The Junior Engineer shook her head. "Nothing." She indicated the apartment, her furniture, the paintings on her walls, the autobar, the books. "Why should I complain? I was born of parents who were both Junior Effectives. I fought my way up this far. I like my work. I am well paid. After only ten years of work I can retire, if I wish, and probably won't wish. The fact of the matter is, I have just about everything I want."

"Except more status," he said bluntly.

"Man does not live by bread alone," she told him bluntly. "I deserve more status. How much status do you deserve, Techno Morris?"

He put his glass down and stood up, his face apologetic. "I'm afraid I've taken up too much of your time, Adele. I should run along." He hesitated and then added, "I don't know what I've done to deserve all this."

She stood too, her expression projecting weariness now. "Nothing," she said. "You're a nice guy. I just got going and it all spilled out. Especially when you told me about your schooling and lack of ambition." She made

98

her moue gain. "I suppose that you'll report all this—to Security."

He grinned at her suddenly. "Why? I'm indebted to you. Remember? I still owe you a drink."

She looked back at him. "I seem to be in a mood to insult my friends tonight. I'll take a rain check on the drink."

13.

Late the following afternoon, Rex Morris drifted into the living room of his uncle's apartment. The older Morris looked up from a tell-screen into which he had been scowling.

"Oh, sorry," Rex said. "Didn't know you were busy. Should I leave?"

"No, no, my boy," the older man said. "I wasn't talking to anyone. I was looking at a book in the Library Data Banks."

"Doing research?" Rex said lightly, dropping onto a couch. "I thought you were more the aging playboy type, Uncle Bill. Wine, women and whistling, rather than book lore."

"None of your lip, youngster. As a matter of fact, I was checking up on the nihilists. Fascinating subject. I don't know how similar this contemporary gang is to the originals but the 19th century nihilists were a determined bunch. More anarchists than anything else, but dedicated. When they decided to eliminate a victim, he might as well have given up and made his will. They kept trying until they got him, by gun, by bomb, by knife—sooner or later they got him. I don't believe they ever operated here in America, more an East European outfit, especially Russia. They finished off various of the old Grand Dukes, especially those who participated in government."

Rex said primly, "I must say, this is rather a controversial subject, isn't it?"

"Come off it, my boy. We're in the seclusion of my home. And certainly you couldn't be Leonard's son without having heard in your time just about anything possible to hear." He switched off the tell-screen, the better to carry on the conversation.

Rex Morris got up from his seat and went over to the autobar and dialed himself a drink, came back and slumped down onto the couch again.

"I suppose that's the point," he said languidly. "The pendulum has swung in the opposite direction. Far as I'm concerned, if I never hear another controversial discussion in my life I'll be just as happy. Where does it get you?"

His uncle looked at him appraisingly. "I don't know whether to believe you or not. At any rate, when you were off on your walk, you had callers."

"Callers? That's too bad. Who in the world would be calling on me?"

"Matt Edgeworth and one of his men. They weren't exactly here for social reasons."

"Edgeworth?" Rex said, scowling puzzlement. "Oh, you mean the Security man. That effective type who seems to have wormed his way into a responsible position. I suppose it could only happen in the Security Functional Sequence. Sort of a brute type."

"Don't underestimate Matt Edgeworth, my boy. He's capable and ambitious in an age when few of us bother to be. A really aggressive man can make his way in any society."

"Well, what did he want? Probably a written guarantee that I wouldn't court Paula Klein. Techna Sims tells me he's down on anybody who gets near enough to Warren Klein's sister to speak to her."

His uncle was shaking his head. "The Security FS is trying to run down the nihilists. Part of their program involves checking out all newcomers to the capital. All hotels, all recently occupied apartments—that sort of thing. They must have their work cut out for them."

"And Edgeworth came to see me?" Rex said. "A Technician running errands?"

"That surprised me too," William Morris said. "However, Edgeworth explained that due to your father's prominence he thought it only fitting that someone of higher rank check you."

Rex snorted. "That didn't seem to apply the other day when he sent that stupid engineer to pick me up for being in a speakeasy."

The older man said slowly, "What are you doing with a secret compartment in your suitcase, Rex?" Before the other could answer, he added. "Technician Edgeworth requested permission to go through your things. Routine, he said. I thought the best policy was to be open and above board and told him you wouldn't at all mind."

"Secret compartment?" Rex said. "Oh, in the alligator bag. I had that made some years ago just before going on a tourist trip to the Australian Technate. Thought I might locate something I might want to sneak through their customs—or ours. Romantic nonsense, eh? I never did use it. What did Edgeworth say?"

"Nothing. There was nothing in it, of course."

"Well, how are they doing with the assassins? What was it you called them?"

"Nihilists. It's stirring up a fantastic mess. I think that the Security FS at first thought to suppress news of the affair. But it buzzed through the speakeasies like a nest of hornets, and then some of the gossip commentators got it into their broadcasts. Absolutely verged on nonconformity. Must have shocked quite a few mental old maids, of both sexes."

"I would think so." Rex said. He took a sip of his drink. "These gossip commentators are a waspish bunch. I'm surprised that the SFS tolerates them. Which reminds me, the other day you dropped a hint that Nadine Sims was . . . how did you put it?"

His uncle squirmed. "She's a beautiful woman, but she's an opportunist, my boy. I had occasion to check up on her on one occasion. Her family are largely junior effectives but she's managed to work her way into Tech-

102

nician circles. I imagine that many of the people she associates with think that she's a Technician caste person herself. She'll probably wind up the wife or mistress of some Technician or even Prime Technician."

"But . . . why?" Rex said in surprise. "Why should she want to go to all that trouble?"

"Don't ask me. For the prestige, I suppose. The desire to be on top. For the sake of being able to enter the Flop House and rub elbows with the Technate's top mucky-mucks."

Rex Morris had emptied his glass. Now he stretched out full length on the couch and relaxed. "A lot of people in this town certainly go to a lot of trouble. Personally, it seems to me that this ambition bit interferes with having a normal good time."

His uncle said peevishly, "Young fellow, it's your type that set off these nihilists."

"My type? My type wouldn't set off anything, Uncle Bill." Rex grinned. "No fire at all."

"That, evidently, is their point. They think the Technate is guilty of suppressing initiative. That incompetents head the country and that consequently progress is being stifled."

Rex yawned and said, "This is getting on the controversial side, isn't it, Uncle Bill?"

His uncle snorted disgust. "When people start shooting at members of our caste it's about time we find out why, Rex. Even a fool protects his life. In a way, I suppose that they're right."

"Great Scott, Uncle Bill!"

"Has it ever occurred to you, Rex, that there is only one living Hero of the Technate? Why, as recently as when I was a boy there must have been a dozen. Your father was the last to gain the honor and that was accomplished more than three decades ago. Since then there has been no service to the Technate performed of sufficient importance to call for the award. Nobody *bleeds* about anything any more."

Rex stifled another yawn. "I suppose that everything of any importance has already been discovered."

His uncle snorted. "Don't be ridiculous, everything will never be discovered. Every time something new is found out, it opens the way to the discovery of still more things."

Rex said with only mild interest, "What's all this about incompetence? Do these murderous malcontents actually suggest that even the Supreme Technician is incompetent?"

"They seem to suggest, my boy, that the whole Techno caste is. That none of us are worth our salt."

Rex grinned again and came to one elbow. "Well, Uncle Bill, I'm evidently going to get into an argument no matter how I try to stay out. So, the truth now. What do you know about teaching, about education and schools?"

His uncle blinked at him. "Don't be ridiculous. I'll let you know I was a good man before my retirement. Why if I'd remained in the Educational Functional Sequence another year or two I undoubtedly would have been appointed Prime Technician."

Rex was still grinning. "You didn't answer me. How good a teacher were you?"

William Morris was indignant. "I entered the EFS as a Senior Engineer, an appointment suitable to my rank. I didn't deal with *teaching*. Anyone of such or above rank is concerned with overall policy, with planning on the higher levels, with . . ."

Rex laughed and leaned back again. "That's what I thought."

The older Morris was indignant. "Look here, my boy, education is more than just teachers and students. Why, one of the last chief executives of the old United States, Eisenhower, before his election to that office, was given the position of president of Columbia, one of the country's largest universities. When the news reporters came to interview him about the appointment, one asked him what background he had for the job. He admitted that he'd had no former connection with education whatsoever and that he would have to be 'briefed' on the subject."

"Well," Rex said, weary of the conversation. "I suppose that's what these nihilists are complaining about.

Here I am, for instance. One of these days someone will appoint me to a Senior Engineer position in Textiles, Entertainment, Medicine, or what-not. I'm as qualified in one field as the other."

His uncle said huffily, "You'll have suitable engineers and effectives to handle the routine work below you."

"That I will and it's all right with me. What's on tonight, Uncle Bill? Are we scheduled for a party or anything? I have half a mind to get thoroughly kinked."

His uncle looked at his watch. "Not for me. I'm becoming progressively interested in this nihilist thing. I think I'll go and check with some of the boys. Find out what's being said on the higher levels. There must have been some new developments by this time."

Rex yawned. "Well, I'll tag along if you don't mind. I suppose I should be spending more time with these friends of yours. Sooner or later one's going to find he needs a promising young Senior Engineer to fill out his sequence, and there I'll be on hand, my bright little face shining."

14.

Down before the apartment house, Rex dialed a two seater hover car and they stood at the curb waiting for it to arrive. When it smoothed up to the curb, Uncle Bill slid behind the manual controls, and to Rex Morris' surprise proceeded to drive the vehicle as though they were on an unautomated road somewhere out in the country.

"Isn't that a little on the dangerous side, Uncle Bill?" he protested mildly. "There's a lot of traffic in this part of town at this time of evening."

His uncle muttered something ambiguous about the Security FS getting excited over the nihilists, and Rex, not getting the connection, gave it up.

They crossed town through the distribution and entertainment centers and emerged into a residential area. William Morris pulled up to a curb, dismissed the car and then led his nephew for a block or two on foot, to the younger man's surprise. They entered a moderately sized apartment building and took one of the elevators to an upper floor. Evidently, the elevator's tell-screen recognized the older Morris, since they were not called upon to identify themselves.

The elevator opened into a small reception hall. They issued forth and paused before a screen there.

"Welcome Technician Morris," a robo-voice said. "Who is your guest?"

"My nephew, Techno Rex Morris," Uncle Bill said impatiently. "I vouch for him, of course."

Rex said, mystified, "What is this a private club? You haven't brought me here before."

"Don't be naive," his uncle told him. "Come along."

A door opened before them and they proceeded into a large room in which a party seemed to be going on. At least, a considerable number of persons stood, or sat about, drinks in hand in the usual cocktail party wise. Several of them called out to William Morris as he and Rex progressed toward the nearest autobar.

There was a small group around the bar and William Morris growled out a humorous protest to them before they made way and let him dial two drinks. He introduced the group to Rex. Two of them were senior engineers, one a full Technician and two others were unassigned Technos like Rex himself. The sixth was a Temple monk.

The Technician said to William Morris, "Here's a point that you might have an opinion on. We're discussing the motivation of these so-called nihilists."

"Yes," the monk said heavily. He was an obese, florid faced man with a small, almost pouting mouth. "The race has never been so happy as today, under the Technate. What do they expect? What is it that they want?"

William Morris jiggled his glass and said tentatively, "What do you mean when you say the race is happy?"

"Well, isn't that obvious?" the monk said. "Past social systems have always had their underprivileged minorities or majorities, for that matter. Even as late as the middle of the 20th century we had large elements of the population even in the United States and Canada who were ill housed, ill clothed and ill fed, lacking in proper medical care and in opportunity for adequate education. Today, no such elements remain. Everyone has all the needs for happy existence."

Uncle Bill took a thoughtful sip of his drink before returning. Then he said, "All the needs for existence, possibly, even healthy existence. But what is happiness? Are we actually any happier now than before?"

107

Rex looked back to the monk.

That worthy was pouting at Uncle Bill. "I don't seem to follow you. How can anybody be happy if he lacks the basic necessities? And today nobody lacks them."

"If what seems to be your definition of happiness applies, then in the old days there was no happiness at all among the poverty stricken, while the rich must have spent their time beaming at each other with joy. And the billionaires, of course, would be hard put to keep from jumping with pure glee."

One of the senior engineers, who'd been sipping at a highball through the discussion thus far, now said, "Wait a minute here. You're not giving us that old jazz about the negroes happily strumming away at their banjos on the levee while the plantation owners, mint juleps in hand, miserably lived in their luxury in the mansions up on the hill?"

One of the unassigned Technos also leaped into the fray. "Yes, just what do you mean by happiness, Technician Morris?"

William Morris grinned at them. "That's a good question. Actually, I don't think there is any such thing." He nodded his head at the Temple monk. "That's the ultimate foolishness of a religion that promises either a heaven or a hell—eternal happiness or eternal sorrow and pain. Neither is possible, neither makes sense, both are contrasts and you can't have the one without the other."

"Now, just a minute," the senior effective protested. "You mean happiness just isn't possible? That's ridiculous. All of us . . ."

"No, now listen," Uncle Bill interrupted. "I don't contend that pleasure, contentment, even ecstacy, aren't possible for comparatively short periods at a time. But a lasting *happiness* just isn't in the cards. The word is meaningless, loosely used, like love. What is love? You love your mother, your wife, your country, and you love apple pie. You even love a parade, though I doubt if you'd want to go to bed with one. Ridiculous! The word means nothing, and neither does the word happiness, except in a temporary sort of way."

"If there is no such thing as happiness," the Temple monk said dryly, "the race has certainly been seeking a will-o'-the-wisp for a long time."

The senior engineer was more heated. "You either haven't said enough, or you just don't know what you're talking about."

Rex's eyes went back to his uncle. The old boy was in fine fettle this afternoon, he decided.

Uncle Bill dialed himself another drink and waited for it, before going on.

"The original question," he said, "was whether our culture is happier now that we've achieved all the essentials for everyone. To illustrate my point, let's go back a bit further in history to 1776 when the American revolutionists were promising Life, Liberty and the Pursuit of Happiness to their undecided fellow subjects of King George. As has been pointed out before, such thinkers as Jefferson and Madison didn't make the mistake of promising *happiness* but merely the opportunity to pursue it. I have a sneaking suspicion that they themselves labored under no misapprehensions about the possibility of it being realized. Two hundred years later a second American revolution evolved and once again happiness was promised, once cradle to the grave abundance was achieved for everyone. Very well, I ask you, are we all happy?"

"We're a damn sight nearer to it than ever before. What could these so-called nihilists even pretend to offer that would improve things?" one of the unassigned Technos said.

Uncle Bill shrugged. "I've never even talked to one of them. Perhaps intellectual stimulation. Perhaps they're tired of sitting around belting booze the way we do most of the time. All our former inventive genius seems today to go into the concoction of ever more exotic mixed drinks."

The senior engineer was more irritated than ever. "What is that supposed to mean?"

Uncle Bill's tone took on an edge of exasperation too. "I'm not contending that the former half starved farmer on a quarter acre of land in India, or a few acres in Indiana, lived a desirable life, nor a worker in a textile mill in 19th century England. Before man can realize himself it's self evident that he needs life's necessities. What I have been trying to put over is that happiness is not the point. Largely man leads a rather monotonous existence, day by day. Sometimes his days are lit by temporary pleasure, even ecstacy, sometimes they are depressed by tragedy, pain, sorrow. These things can happen to either rich or poor.

"The important thing is that the man who has all life's necessities in abundance can lead a more *full* life. His health is more often good, he had leisure to pursue hobbies, or studies or physical pleasures. He more often has prestige in the community, whether or not he deserves it. He has a better chance of being adjusted to the world as he finds it. Surely life is better with all these things. But they don't assure this elusive thing happiness."

Uncle Bill finished his second drink and came to a conclusion. "However, so far as I can learn about these nihilists, based on the threatening letters they've been writing, they aren't dealing with happiness at all. They seem to think our culture is stagnating under a hierarchal social system and they want to set it into motion again by some basic changes."

"What changes?" the monk pouted.

"Search me," Uncle Bill shrugged. He turned to say something to his nephew and found that Rex Morris had taken off.

The younger Morris, glass in hand, was on the other side of the room, taking in a conversation at a table. It was even more heated than the one in which his uncle was engaged. Rex Morris was mildly surprised. Some club.

A thin engineer was snapping, "What do you mean democracy failed? We've never bothered to try it. Certainly not since primitive society, when government was based on the clan, and they practiced a primitive type of communism. Since then we've periodically payed lip service to democracy and that's about all. Democracy in Athens during the so called Golden Age? Bosh. Sure, the Athe-

110

nian citizen had it, but for every citizen there was a flock of slaves who had no word in the government at all. The United States? Ha! once again. Our ancestors talked a good case of democracy but that was about it. In its early days in the eighteenth and nineteenth centuries there were property and educational requirements that disenfranchised a majority of the population. For that matter, until after the First World War women couldn't vote at all. I won't even mention the discrimination against Negro and other minority groups that lasted right up until the founding of the Technate. But above all, real democracy was impossible as long as you had economic autocracy. How can a man freely exercise his vote when he is economically dependent upon someone else?"

"I don't get that," somebody said.

"What could be more obvious? If you're dependent upon someone else for your food, clothing and shelter, you aren't free. A child, dependent upon his parents, isn't free. The family is a dictatorship, a benevolent one, but still a dictatorship. Neither is a man who sells his time to another free, not when his basic needs of life are dependent upon the selling. So I ask the question again. How can you have a political democracy when you have an economic autocracy? When the means of production are owned and operated by and for a minority? We never gave real democracy a chance, and then, when we established the Technate, we gave such democratic institutions as we did have their death blow."

Rex Morris whistled quietly between his teeth. He looked about the room, covetly. There were possibly seventy-five people, none lower in rank than Senior Engineer.

He saw someone he recognized and went over and said, "I understand that you and I are waging a feud."

Paula Klein, attired today in a Technician gray suit, the severity of which only emphasized her brunette beauty, said coldly, "Did you ever hear the term stool pigeon, Techno Morris?" Her dark eyes flashed her disdain.

"I don't think so," Rex said in a rueful tone. "It doesn't sound so very good."

She said bitingly, "My brother didn't appreciate the fact that you reported that I'd taken you to an effective caste speakeasy, unbeknownst to yourself."

"Look," he tried to explain. "You had already told me that the Security Functional Sequence engineer out in front of that place had recognized you. Great Scott, he even saluted. And, besides, the fact that some spy turned me in was an indication that everyone there had been spotted. There was no possible way for me to have defended you."

She frowned at him.

He said urgently, "If I'd been brought into a Technocourt the whole thing would have been made public. What else made sense for me to do? As it was, we both escaped that embarrassment."

She looked at him for a long speculative moment. "Well," she sighed. "I can't exactly agree with your reasoning, Techno Morris, but you do put some sort of light on it."

He grinned at her. "Let's start all over again. How about a drink?"

"You forget, I'm the one person in a million that doesn't slug it down these days. How in the world did you ever get in here, Rex?"

"Oh, Uncle Bill brought me. He's been making a point of introducing me to all his friends. I'm in no hurry for an appointment, but I suppose that the sooner I put in my ten years, the sooner I can retire and live life the way it should be lived."

"And how is that? Do you have some particular hobby, or some subject you study?"

"Ummm, that I have. Wine, women and wandering about enjoying myself. Not necessarily in that order. Which brings to mind that I saw you at the Flop House the night before last. You *do* go to spots other than speakeasies then. And don't seem to have any more suitable escorts than that Matt Edgeworth clod. How about taking pity on a stranger and devoting an evening to exploring the town?"

Her face was expressionless, she had frozen up again.

112

She said evenly, "I am afraid that spending time with you, Techno Morris, is somewhat of a hazard. Suppose one of the Security men here this afternoon reports our presence? I'm afraid that in your mad rush to alibi yourself I might wind up . . ."

"Security men?" Rex said. "Why should there be any security men here. And, even if there were, what of it?"

She said bitterly, "Did you think it was effective class speakeasies only that they cover? Believe me, they are also in engineer caste and technician as well. I doubt if there's a speakeasy in town that Matt Edgeworth doesn't know about."

Rex Morris said blankly, "You mean to tell me that this is a speakeasy and that there are Security FS men here?"

She looked at him as though he was mad. "Where in the name of Good Howard did you think you were? Where did you imagine your uncle had brought you? Did you think that only the effectives went to speakeasies?"

"Great Scott," Rex Morris blurted. "I thought it was, well, sort of a club. Uncle Bill has introduced me to a half dozen clubs here in Greater Washington. I *did* think they were talking rather loosely, but then I'm from the sticks and this is the capital city. But, a *speakeasy!*"

She shook her head at him cynically. "And this is the son of Leonard Morris?"

He was snappish. "Stop saying that! I'm sick of being the son of somebody."

"I wonder how he feels about you," she said contemptuously. Paul Klein turned on her heel and stalked off.

Rex Morris stared after her for a long moment, and let out his breath unhappily. Great Scott she was one of the most attractive young women he had ever met, and they had so many things in common potentially that he didn't dare begin to count them. He was thirty, and thus far in life had never met his woman. Paula Klein was potentially his woman. But it was too late now.

He turned and, deliberately avoiding the vicinity of his uncle, made his way through the crowded room to the reception hall which they had entered earlier. As he progressed, he picked up a snatch of conversation or argument here and there. Most of the groups were discussing the nihilists and their threat.

In the reception room he had no difficulty in getting an elevator to take him to the street level.

He walked down the street and to the nearest public tell-screen. He stood before it and said, "Technician Matt Edgeworth of the Security Functional Sequence."

A robo voice said, "Carried out," and there was a pause.

An engineer in Security FS uniform appeared on the screen and said, "What was the subject of your call to the Technician, please? I am one of his assistants."

Rex Morris rasped, "I wish to report an openly operating speakeasy."

"Oh?" the other said, not exactly overwhelmed by the statement. "I can take that information."

Rex Morris rapped, "I'd rather report the matter to Technician Edgeworth himself."

"Why? I am afraid Technician Edgeworth is busy. As you must realize his duties are numerous."

"Well, busy or not, tell him that Techno Rex Morris wants to speak to him." He added bitterly, "The son of Hero of the Technate Leonard Morris."

The security officer's eyes widened. "Sorry, Techno Morris. I had no idea of your identity. Carried out, immediately."

His face faded to be replaced shortly by that of a scowling Matt Edgeworth. "Yes?" he said. "What can I do for you Techno Morris?"

Rex said, "Others seem to be continually dragging me into these confounded speakeasies. This time I thought I'd report directly to you before somebody else did."

"Indeed," the heavyset security head said. "Where were you taken, and by whom."

Rex gave him the address and the floor number of the oversized apartment, converted into a speakeasy. The other didn't seem particularly impressed.

"And just who was it that took you to this place?"

"I'd . . . I'd rather not say."

114

Matt Edgeworth looked at him.

Rex Morris cleared his throat. He said unhappily, "As a matter of fact, it was my uncle, William Morris."

"I see," Edgeworth said. "Very well, the matter will be taken care of, Techno Morris." The tell-screen went blank.

Rex Morris stared at it for awhile, reflectively, then shifted his shoulders and went back to the street. There was a Transport FS box on the corner and he summoned a one seater hover cab.

He spent the next quarter of an hour driving up and down in the main streets of Greater Washington haphazardly. It became obvious, eventually, that he wasn't being followed, or, if so, by someone so accomplished that he wasn't to be detected.

He headed for another part of town, to a residential section largely devoted to effective class apartments. He dismissed the car a full half mile from his destination and walked from the point. His gray, Techno caste suit made him somewhat conspicuous in this vicinity but not to any dangerous extent. He looked up and down the street before entering the building of his destination.

There was an elevator, but he walked up the stairs to the third floor where he let himself into a small effective caste flat. He went into the bedroom and began to strip off his clothing. He looked over at the autobar and for a moment considered dialing himself a drink, but then shook his head. He'd had two drinks at his uncle's speakeasy and under the circumstances that was enough. The drinking pace he'd had to assume as a supposed live-it-up playboy in this fast paced city had been far and beyond his usual intake and he didn't appreciate it in view of his present position.

He went into the bedroom, clad in his underclothing, hung his suit in the closet and took down effective caste jumper and trousers, put them on and then returned to the living room.

He went to a closet, fishing an old fashioned key from his pocket. He unlocked it, opened the door and pushed aside various standard articles of clothing to reveal a small, long chest. This involved another key. He opened it and hunkered down on his heels and stared thoughtfully.

There were two handguns, a sawed-off shotgun, an old fashioned carbine with a telescope and three hand grenades. He took up one of the handguns and clicked the magazine from the butt and examined it. He ejected the cartridges one by one and tested the strength of the magazine's spring. If you allowed an automatic's magazine to remain full for too long a period, the spring sometimes weakened to the point that the last two or three cartridges weren't fed into the barrel. However, the spring seemed strong enough. He fed the slugs back into the magazine and jammed it back into the butt of the gun and then jacked the first cartridge into firing position. He flicked the safety on.

However, he thought about it some more and finally slipped the weapon into his belt and picked up one of the grenades and hefted it. It would ring in a new element, a bomb rather than a bullet. There was something more dramatic about a bomb. You usually connected nihilists and anarchists with bombs. Why, he had no idea. But hadn't the Archduke Ferdinand been finished off with a bomb, thus precipitating the First World War?

He put the deadly thing in a side pocket, relocked the chest, came to his feet and relocked the closet door. He grunted sour self deprecation. All this use of locks and keys was probably nonsense. If this hideaway of his was located, a couple of locks were not going to deter any searchers.

Nevertheless, he carefully locked the door of the apartment upon leaving. At least he wouldn't have the bad luck of any kids or prowlers stumbling upon his weapons cache. He took the stairs down to the street level, again avoiding the use of the elevator.

He walked several blocks before summoning a cab at a Transport FS box, but then caught himself before climbing in. Confound it, he had almost forgotten himself. His Universal Credit Card was that of a Techno, but he wore effective caste clothing. A Techno rode free but an effec-

116

tive must use his credit card. If he climbed into this cab, the cab's screen would note his clothing and expect payment. If he brought forth his Techno card, the off-beat information would undoubtedly be flashed to the computers. Technician rank persons didn't make a practice of going about in effective clothing. It wasn't illegal but it simply wasn't done.

Damn it. He would have to forego the cab.

Rex Morris went, instead, to the nearest metro entrance and descended to the traffic level. He sought out on the wall map the nearest station to his destination and took an automated twenty-seater to it, after putting his Universal Credit Card in the appropriate slot. He knew this would be safe, since there was no tell-screen here. No ergs would be deduced from his account, since he was a Techno, but it was necessary to identify himself to get through the turnstile.

The twenty-seater had him to his destination in a matter of minutes.

He left the metro, orientated himself and strolled along the sidewalk unobtrusively. Unbeknownst to his uncle, or anyone else who might have been aware of his identity, Rex Morris had spent several periods in Greater Washington learning the ins and outs of the city, and performing various other matters in preparation for his present activities.

He reached the Central Shrine Temple and looked up at its soaring towers, but kept walking. It was dark by now. He circled the monstrous building to the extensive park behind it. At this hour, there were few pedestrians about.

He walked along the park path which paralleled a tall iron picket fence until he reached a small iron gate. He looked up and down. The spot was quite secluded, as he knew from past checking. Nobody was in sight. Rex Morris dipped into his pocket and came forth with a compact tool. He opened it and inserted it into the gate's lock. He twisted sharply. There was no result and he swore under his breath and darted another look up and down the walk. It was still deserted, thank God.

117

He twisted the tool in the other direction and felt, rather than heard, a click. He pushed the gate open. He hurried through, closed the gate behind him, and disappeared into the shrubbery on the other side.

Now it was in the lap of the gods. He had carefully studied everything he could find about the schedule of his victim but he realized full well that it was a far cry from what appeared in the mass media about a prominent personage and the real life that the celebrity lived.

He worked his way through the shrubbery and garden to the official residence, stood in the shelter of a tree and waited more or less patiently. If he had it right, he wouldn't have to wait more than a half hour. If he had it wrong, he'd simply have to come back another night and that would have its complications since he had broken the simple lock on that gate and sooner or later, and probably sooner, some gardener, or whoever, was going to discover it.

As a matter of fact, now that he thought about it, if he wasn't able to accomplish his mission tonight, he'd better never return. With this nihilist hunt on, they'd be posting Security Functional Sequence men all over town.

It was agonizing standing here doing nothing. He wondered, unhappily, what would happen if a Security FS officer came through the park and noted the gate was openable. But then he shifted his shoulders in self disgust. Ridiculous. Even if an officer did pass, he'd have no reason to suspect the broken lock. The gate was seemingly closed as it usually was. It was extremely unlikely that anyone would touch it.

There was a movement in the room he was watching. Rex Morris stiffened in anticipation. Lights went on.

He brought the grenade from his pocket. It was a high explosive, concussion type he had picked up several years ago on a supposed tourist trip to Egypt. You could buy anything in Egypt, given sufficient international credit at your disposal. There was a selective device that allowed the detonator to be set at three seconds, ten seconds, or five minutes after the pulling of the pin. He set it at five minutes, got down on his hands and knees and crept toward the window.

It was summer. Summers in Greater Washington are humid and hot as the corridors of hell. If what he had read was correct, his victim did not like airconditioning. The window should be ajar.

It was.

They were making preparations inside. Two of them, garbed in simple Temple robes, setting the table for an evening meal. He grunted sour amusement to note the wine carafe. Supposedly, his victim was an abstainer of ten given to speaking against alcohol.

He waited, grenade in hand. He had to depend on guesswork now, and he couldn't make a mistake. His mouth worked, anxiety high. There was so much at stake. He simply couldn't afford to make a mistake. He would never forgive himself.

The two left the room, obviously temporarily.

He pulled the grenade's pin, shoved the window slightly more open, tossed the small bomb in and under a side table, then pulled the window back into the same position it had been in before. He turned and scurried back to the shelter of the shrubbery.

He peered, eyes narrowed, up and down, cursed silently when he made out a young couple, arms about waists, strolling slowly along the walk.

They were walking so slowly, so very very slowly, that for all practical purposes they were stopped as far as he was concerned.

In fact, now they did stop and went into a huddle.

This was not going to be a hasty kiss. That was obvious.

Rex Morris groaned and shot a look back at the residence. He was going to have to risk it. Without looking left or right, he briskly walked over to the gate. He opened it and went on through. He closed it behind him and walked briskly past the two lovers.

They didn't even see him.

He held himself from running, or even walking so fast

that it would be noticeable. He was to the edge of the park before the explosion. He ignored it, crossed the street and headed for the metro station, still walking briskly but not overly so.

15.

Rex Morris was late in coming down to breakfast in the morning but his uncle was waiting for him. And it was not the usually good natured Uncle Bill.

The older man said, his voice dangerously low, "You didn't bother to say goodbye when you left me yesterday."

"No, I didn't," Rex said, a defiant element in his voice rather than apology. "I wanted to talk to you about that."

"And I to you," his uncle said. "Start talking."

"Well, frankly . . . well, Great Scott Uncle Bill, do you think you ought to be going into places like that? Not to speak of taking me. I don't even have an appointment yet. I'll never get a decent one if word goes around that I'm carrying on Dad's non-conformist ways. You know that, Uncle Bill."

"Leave your father out of it," his uncle snapped. "I don't agree with some of his extreme views, but Leonard was always a *man*."

"I don't like the way you say that. I've got a right to my own opinions and one of them is that the Technate shouldn't allow these cesspools of uncontrolled controversy. Why, there was even a Temple monk at that place yesterday. How can the Technate remain on an even keel when every institution we have is being attacked?"

His uncle growled, "I'm beginning to wonder if we haven't been on an even keel for too damn long. But right now, that isn't the point, Rex Morris. The point is that after I'd taken you into that club . . ."

"That speakeasy!"

". . . yesterday, you left and reported it to the Security FS."

"What did you expect me to do?" Rex blurted. "I am a loyal Techno."

William Morris stared at him for a long moment. He shook his head. "So you don't deny it, eh? The second generation. The son of Leonard Morris, the non-conformist."

Rex Morris said heatedly, "I told you where I stood. I'm not interested in being the son of Leonard Morris. All I want is to take my rightful position in the Technate. Get a decent appointment, put in my ten years of service, then retire and devote myself to enjoying life. That's *all* I want."

His uncle said flatly, "You're old enough to make your own decisions and I'd be the last to rally to the cause of non-conformism. I stop in at a speakeasy once in a blue moon, just for the amusement, just to see what goes on. Nevertheless, I don't want anyone in my home who turns me in to the Security FS in a panic because he's afraid his reputation might be tarnished by association with such as me. No thank you."

Rex flushed. "Does that mean. . . .?"

"It does, indeed. Explain it to your father, however you wish, but you are no longer welcome here, Rex Morris."

"I'll get my things together and leave immediately," Rex said.

"Take your time, Rex."

In his room, before packing, Rex Morris went over to the tell-screen and said into it, "Housing Functional Sequence, please."

The robo voice said, "Carried out," and the screen lit up.

A desk faded in, behind it a junior effective. She looked at him and smiled. "Yes, sir."

Rex said, "I'm Rex Morris, unassigned Techno, Serial One-224A-1326, waiting for an appointment in this city. I would like an adequate single apartment." He added, "In a part of town suited to my rank, of course."

"Of course," she said. "Serial One, you said. May I have the rest of that, again, please?"

He gave it to her and she dialed the full identification code on an instrument on her desk and a card slid into view on a smaller screen before her.

Impressed, she said, "Techno Morris, could I suggest that you stay at one of the better hotels until you have found adequate quarters? We'll assign an effective to your needs at once. He will be able to devote full time to your needs and should have you adequately established in . . ."

Rex said impatiently, "I'm not as difficult to please as all that. I'd like a place to go to immediately. Something that is available this morning. If I'm unsatisfied, I'll check with you later, but I'm sure I will be."

"Very well, Techno Morris," she said hurriedly. "I'll check immediately. She went through various other motions, made two quick calls then turned to him again, a pleased smile on her face. "I think I have just the place for you, sir." She gave him an address and an apartment number.

He packed his things into his three bags, placed them in the servo compartment of the room, turned to the tellscreen again and said, "Have the things in the servo delivered to this address." He looked down at the paper on which he had noted his new apartment number and read it off.

The robo said, "Carried out."

Rex left, not bothering to look up his uncle for a final farewell. He suspected that the less the old boy saw of him in the immediate future the better William Morris would like it. There was a rueful smile faint on his lips as he left the apartment behind. Of all the people in the world, his uncle was very near the top of those that Rex Morris loved.

16.

The new apartment was fine enough, as he knew it would be. Not as elaborate as that of his Uncle Bill, but certainly ample for a young bachelor. He unpacked, had himself a short drink and thought it all out some more. So far, his campaign was running to plan and on schedule but he couldn't afford to risk letting his defences slip, to run the chance of blowing his cover.

He went to Nadine Sims apartment that afternoon without calling her in advance, other, of course, than requesting her apartment of the elevator robo. When he stepped into her reception room, however, she was awaiting him, a questioning smile on her face, two glasses in her hands.

"Surprise, surprise," she said. "I wasn't expecting you." She offered him one of the glasses.

"If this is a John Brown's Body, no thanks," Rex said to her. "You worked that particular wile on me the other night. Was I kinked before the evening was through."

"You were? Good Howard, all that uproar about the nihilists sobered me up. Anyway, this is a Rattlesnake. You said you went for them in your part of the Technate. You see, I'm being apologetic for running off the other night, especially since you had been so knightly in taking me to the Flop House."

Rex took the glass. "A Rattlesnake," he said easily. "I

haven't seen one since I left Taos. What a memory the girl has." He followed her into the living room.

"The better to spider you into my web," Nadine Sims said, lifting one well shaped eyebrow in a mock sinister leer.

"Ah ha, so that's the pitch. I'm plied with Rattlesnakes so you can do your will on me, in spite of my youth."

She made him comfortable in a deep chair which sported a built-in autobar and hookah, sat down across from him and eyed him quizzically. She said lightly, "You're making for quite a bit of gossip these days, my lad from the wild west."

He sighed and tried the drink. "Oh! Well, that's just what I don't want but it doesn't seem to do me any good. I'm just a simple country boy, but I seem continually to be dragged into things by you sophisticates of the big city."

She laughed at him, shook her head in disbelief. "If you don't want gossip, I'd suggest you not pull such capers as reporting to the Security FS a speakeasy in which your uncle and half his friends are having a grand time arguing about the most controversial subjects imaginable."

Rex stared at her. "Great Scott, how could you know that, especially this soon?"

She chuckled at him and shook her head again. "Rex, my dear, you have no idea how gossip ridden a capital city can be. The whole matter was on the air not half an hour after it happened, cleverly hidden in hints and innuendoes, of course, but anyone in the know could puzzle it out."

He grunted, and took a slug of his drink. "Well, did any of the commentators mention the fact that Uncle Bill politely booted me out of his home today?"

Her eyes were suddenly more narrow, her face more serious. "Oh, no. You don't mean permanently? Your uncle is one of the most popular men in town. You'll never get into such spots as the Techno-Casino and the Flop House if you've antagonized him."

He finished his drink, dialed another from the chair,

while saying, "Well, consider him antagonized. I don't care. I wish the hell people would stop sucking me into situations in which I'm not interested." He added sourly, "Am I the only object of gossip in town these days? What else is going on?"

She took a sip of her drink, thoughtfully. "You come under the head of light news," she said, her voice less warm now. "The big item is the progress of the nihilist gang. Evidently, they're stronger than was first thought. Stronger and more vicious. They made an attempt on the Supreme Bishop of the Temple last night."

"The *Supreme Bishop!*" Rex blurted. His eyes widened as though in disbelief.

"A bomb," she said. "Thrown into his dining room. His Serenity escaped, but one of his retainers, one of the monks, was hit by flying fragments."

"Killed?" Rex asked quickly.

"Well, no. Barely wounded."

Rex Morris shook his head. "And people think it's strange I'm so indignant about the speakeasies. No wonder outfits like the nihilists develop with half the people in town saying the most controversial things possible. Talk about them and sooner or later you start doing them —that's what I say."

"Do you?" Nadine Sims yawned. "Well, to what do I owe this pleasant visit, Techno Morris?"

He looked at her, surprised. "I beg your pardon?"

"I have plans for this evening," she told him. "I wondered if there was anything special you came to see me about." She looked at her watch.

He came to his feet suddenly and laughed. "I get it."

She stood too, put her drink down on a handy table and stepped over to him, her eyes wide. "Now don't be silly, Rex. I simply have an appointment."

He said, amusement in his voice. "Of course you do. Someone, I assume, who'll take you to the Hush Puppy Room, the Casino, or perhaps the Flop House—or one of the other prestige joints where effectives on the make usually aren't allowed."

Her hand came up and smacked him fiercely across the

127

lower face. She raised the other hand for another swing, but he caught it roughly. He grinned sourly down into her eyes. "Truth hurts, eh? you cheap opportunist," he growled.

"You soft headed, soft living snob," she snarled. "Let go of my hand."

"How you do go on," he said, dropping it. He turned and headed for the door.

"Don't bother to come back," she snapped after him.

He grinned over his shoulder at her. "The sea is loaded with fish like you, sweetie."

17.

At the curb before her house he twisted his mouth in silent thought. Was he pushing things too fast? For the first time since his arrival in the capital he wished he had someone with whom to consult. The things he was doing weighed heavily upon him. Well, forget about it. That was a luxury he could not afford—a confident.

He walked toward the center of the city, turning several streets with little traffic either hover car or pedestrian. It became obvious, after a time that he wasn't being followed.

He summoned a hover car, threw it onto manual control and headed for the section of town he had been in the day before. Once again, he dismissed the vehicle half a mile or so from his destination and finished the trip on foot. Safety, Rex Morris had decided long ago was a matter of taking infinite pains.

He walked up to the small effective caste apartment, let himself in and sank into an easy chair. He dialed himself a weak Irish and water and sat sipping it while he thought out his next campaign.

The drink tasted terrible. He went into the bath and poured the balance of it into the bowl, then went back into the living room and stood in its center trying to come to a decision.

Well, one evening was as good as another, and he

wanted to keep matters at a white heat. He strode with quick decision to the closet, opened it and pushed the clothing impatiently to one side, fishing the key from his pocket to open the hidden chest.

He opened it and stared down at his small arsenal.

A mocking voice from behind him said, "Ah, our nihilist inspects his weapons."

Rex Morris' hand dipped quickly into the chest, emerged with a short barrelled Parabellum. He twirled, the gun at the ready, his lips thinned back over his teeth.

Matt Edgeworth stood at the door, his thumbs tucked into the corners of his uniform jacket pockets. His rugged face wore a cynical twist. He ignored the other's gun, closed the door behind him, made his way to the middle of the room and lowered his bulk into a chair next to the autobar. He leaned forward and dialed himself a drink. While Rex watched him, still unbelieving, the bar delivered a long glass of dark brew.

"Stout," Matt Edgeworth told him. "Very proletarian, eh? Sometimes I think I'm the last of the proletarians." He chuckled and looked down at the insignia marks of technician rank of his Security FS uniform.

Rex Morris walked back, confronting the other, his gun trained and ready. He said tightly, "I suppose your men are knee deep about the place?"

"To the contrary," Edgeworth said easily. "I came alone. Why should I share the prestige of having captured the notorious nihilist? Especially since the said desperate criminal is also the son of an overly publicized Hero of the Technate."

"You can leave my father out of this. Anything I've done is on me alone. Forget about Leonard Morris."

"It's all right with me," Edgeworth said lazily, sipping his dark beer. "I always did think he was overrated. A couple of years work in a laboratory and he's a tin hero for the rest of his life."

The Parabellum was trained at the other's belt buckle. Rex Morris said tightly, "You seem to have a lot of confidence for someone who's covered. Is there any particular reason?"

Matt Edgeworth's voice turned sour. "How long do you think you could have continued narrowly missing your supposed victims before someone caught on to the fact that this generation's breed of assassins hasn't got the guts to really kill anybody?"

Rex Morris' jaw tightened and the finger on the trigger of the gun whitened.

Matt Edgeworth came to his feet. His right hand darted out with surprising speed considering tne man's size and chopped at the other's wrist. The gun fell to the floor. Edgeworth ignored it and sat down again.

He said, conversationally, "Was it really loaded? Have a seat old man, and lets have a little talk about nihilists. Drink?"

Rex glared at him, dialed another Irish whiskey and sank down into the chair across from his unwanted guest. "How'd you find me?" he growled.

Edgeworth shrugged his heavy shoulders. "You know," he said easily, "that's a popular fancy that seems to have come down through the centuries. The mistaken belief that the police are on the stupid side. Believe me, *Techno* Morris, they aren't."

He began to enumerate on his fingers. "One, you're the son of the controversial Leonard Morris, so obviously we'd keep track of you. Two, the nihilist letters began appearing after your arrival. Three, you were just a little too precious in the way you avoided anything controversial. Four, you slugged a Security man who was tagging you. Five, the night of the so-called assassination attempt on Warren Klein, something happened to one of the agents who were trailing you; he was doped at his post. You have an alibi for the time involved which is something I don't quite understand, however it doesn't explain the doped agent. Six, you were just *too* much of a heel in exposing both Paula Klein and your uncle when they did a bit of innocent attending of speakeasies. Seven . . . Do we really need a seven? For that matter, we have an eight, nine and ten."

Rex Morris grunted his self disgust. "An amateur

doing a professional's job," he said bitterly. "Shall we go? I suppose that I'm under arrest."

"Oh, not yet," the Security Technician said easily. "Let's talk awhile. Where did you get your arsenal? The rifle, these guns you have here, the grenades?"

"Mostly out of private gun collections around Taos," Rex said. "Over a period of years. The grenades, I bought abroad, in Egypt. I pretended to be a collector."

"No accomplices, eh?"

"None."

"Well, we'll find out about that later," Edgeworth said, nodding his head and taking another pull at his drink. "For instance, I'm interested in how you got the use of two effective caste apartments, this one and the one from which you took a shot at Warren Klein. Although I suppose it was no great problem, you probably simply subleased them under an assumed name. But tell me, just what did you have in mind with the whole farce?"

"Tell *me* something first," Rex growled. "How did you find me here? I didn't detect you following me. You or anybody else."

Edgeworth grinned his contempt. "Dip your hand into your jacket pocket. I don't know if it would be the right pocket, or left."

Mystified, Rex plunged his hands into his pockets. One of them came out with a button sized object he couldn't remember ever having seen before.

"Transmitter," Edgeworth grinned at him. "Why follow you about the streets when you've been planted with a nice little broadcasting station that can notify me just where you are, just any time at all? The moral of the story is not to get too close to a girl."

Rex blinked down at the little electronic device, and then looked up at the Security man uncomprehendingly, but then it came to him and he blurted, "Nadine Sims."

The other raised his heavy eyebrows. "Please. You mean Senior Engineer of the Security FS, Nadine Sims. Let's have correct rank here, *Techno* Morris." Edgeworth turned back to the autobar and dialed a fresh drink, after tossing his first glass into a corner. "Now, once again, *why?* Just what did you have in mind with all this silly masquerade and phony heroics?"

"The overthrow of the Technate!" Rex snapped back.

Technician Edgeworth stared at him for a moment, then threw his head back and began to laugh. "All by yourself, you pipsqueak? The overthrow of the Technate! How, in the name of Veblen? By *almost* shooting a few upper rank Technos?"

Rex Morris took a deep breath and stared down at the floor. "An amateur. . . ." he repeated. He looked up at the other. "No," he said. "I didn't expect to do it all myself. All I hoped to accomplish was to set people thinking again. Give them a shot in the arm, a mental jolt. A realization that it was possible that the Technate wasn't necessarily the best of all possible worlds and that it might be worth considering alternatives."

"I don't seem to follow your reasoning. So far, you've made precious little sense."

Rex shrugged his despair. "We've been in a rut for generations. Whatever happened to such ambitions as the conquest of space, as the improvement of the race by controlled genetics, as the eventual attainment of . . . of the Godhead? At first the Technate seemed to be a step in advance, but it bogged down into a rut like that the Egyptians were in for millennia. I hoped to start a controversy, to start people thinking, to make them afraid, to . . . well, stir things up."

"Your father had nothing to do with this, eh?" Edgeworth asked. "Didn't know about this crackpot plan?"

"Nothing at all," Rex said earnestly.

Matt Edgeworth thought about that for awhile. He said slowly, "I think perhaps things would be better if he did."

Rex Morris stared at him, uncomprehending. "But I just told you. He knows nothing about it."

Matt Edgeworth said musingly, "I think the nihilist threat would be even more impressive if we revealed that a Hero of the Technate was involved. Who knows? Perhaps we'll find that a few other notables—your uncle, perhaps—are also in it."

Rex Morris snorted his contempt. "You'll have a hard

time proving that in a Technocourt. Once I appear, I'll tell the whole story and I can prove every point. I did it all myself."

"Uh huh," the other said thoughtfully. "And such a trial would give you a bang up opportunity to make your little speech. To make a martyr of yourself. A little hero all of your own. In fact, there's nothing you'd like better than such a trial, is there *Techno* Morris?"

Rex said nothing.

Edgeworth twisted his face in his characteristic grimace. "Well, don't count too much on having one."

Rex looked up sharply. "Just what do you mean by that?"

"I mean," the other said coldly, "that you have precious little chance, *Techno* Morris, of ever getting into court. I'm afraid that we'll be confronted with the need of, ah, eliminating you, perhaps whilst you make your third assassination attempt. Come to think of it, possibly *after* you've made your attempt. Who knows, this time you might even be successful in another crack at Warren Klein."

Rex shook his head in lack of understanding. "I don't see what motivates you," he said.

Matt Edgeworth slipped a handgun from an underarm holster and trained it on the other. He said, "Some of the things you've said are correct. A change is called for. Sooner or later it'll be made—I assume. But after me, if there is anything I can do about it. You're playing with revolution, *Techno* Morris. Do you know what that can mean? Have you ever seen pictures from the old days of former dictators, police agents, even minor officials, hanging by their heels from lamposts? Do you know what volcanos can be stirred up by social forces once unleashed? No thank you. After me the deluge, perhaps, but if there's anything I can do about it, not until *after* me."

He was warming to his subject. "Right now the Technate is lax, partly because you hereditary Technos are too spineless, too soft. We need a stronger Security FS. Fine, I'm willing to provide it. With this feather in my cap, the crushing of the nihilists, I'll be slated for the Congress of

134

Prime Technicians. Once there—who knows? The Prime Technician of the Security FS is no minor role. We've never had a Supreme Technician from this Functional Sequence, but why not set the precedent?"

"You?" Rex laughed at him. "You become Supreme Technician? On the ambitious side, aren't you Edgeworth?"

Edgeworth glowered at him, bleakly. "There've been ambitious men come to the top before, *Techno* Morris, and the hierarchy is the ideal governmental form to expedite the matter. As an effective born, you probably look on me as lacking in education, but, believe me, I've looked into this particular subject. You ever hear of Atahualpa?"

Rex scowled at him. "The last of the Incas?"

"That's right. Remember what happened to the Incas in Peru? Their society was a primitive equivalent of our Technate, with the Inca at the very top, instead of a Supreme Technician. When Francisco Pizarro landed, all he had to do was kidnap, and later kill, Atahualpa, and the whole machinery of government fell into his hands. A few score strong, ambitious men seized a quarter of all South America." He grunted his contempt. "Do you think wishy-washy milksops like Warren Klein and such hereditary Technos are going to stand in the way of *men*, like me?" There was a fanatical note in his voice now that Rex Morris hadn't noticed before.

Rex said, "You really hate us Technos by birth, don't you Edgeworth?"

"I got to my position the hard way," the other said. "The way the Technate was originally meant to run."

Rex Morris said, "And I suppose if you got to the top —and I assume you have a gang you'd take along with you—then the old system of nepotism and favoritism wouldn't continue, eh? *Your* son would never get any further than effective rank, unless he really qualified, eh?"

"We'll see about that when the time comes," Edgeworth said flatly. He stood and-motioned with the gun. "Let's go now. I've got a lot to arrange."

Rex stood too and began to turn, as though heading

135

for the door, then he took a deep breath, spun and plunged toward the Security man.

Breath whooshed from Matt Edgeworth's massive body as the smaller man's arms went around his waist. The gun clattered to the floor and the two of them fell atop of it, for the moment a confusion of arms and legs akimbo.

Edgeworth's roar held more of disgust, than rage. "Why, you little pipsqueak!" He pounded short jabs into Rex Morris' ribs, began rolling atop the other crushingly.

Morris' mouth worked in a silent prayer to some unbelieved in diety, as he managed to squirm his right hand into his jacket pocket. He was rapidly losing control under the heavier man's pounding blows, but he shook his head for clarity. He made a supreme effort, grabbed at the other desperately, rubbed his index finger and thumb over Matt Edgeworth's naked hand.

He groaned, "All right, I've had it."

Edgeworth came to his feet and gave the other a quick kick in the ribs in a fury. "That was a fool trick," he snarled. "I've got fifty pounds on you and the training of a Security effective as well. Another couple of minutes and you'd have been enjoying a set of broken bones, *Techno* . . ."

The big Security official's voice suddenly fell away. His eyes glazed. He froze in his standing position.

Rex Morris stood up, allowed himself another brief groan for the sake of heavy blows taken. He looked at the stricken Edgeworth and muttered, "Thanks Dad, although I doubt if you ever figured on that instant anesthetic discovery of yours ever being used for this purpose."

He hurried to the bathroom, washed his fingers quickly. It took time, but it was possible for the paralyzing drug to seep through even the heaviest skin.

He returned to the living room, moving rapidly. He took up Matt Edgeworth's hand weapon and stuffed it into his belt. He felt the other over and emerged with a wallet. Inside was an identification card for the Security F.S. Technician. Rex Morris hesitated momentarily, then pocketed it.

He had about thirty minutes to go before Edgeworth

snapped out of the coma. For a long moment he stared at the Security man, even got to the point of taking the gun out again and thumbing back the safety release.

But no. A life time's conditioning isn't to be fluffed away that quickly. He pushed the weapon back into his belt and hurriedly left the room.

Within the half hour, the search would be under way. He was in the clutch now. He was on the run.

There are few places to which to run in a completely integrated society.

18.

There had been something that Edgeworth had said. It hadn't struck a spark by itself, but it had combined with other combustible material. Possibly, just possibly, Rex Morris had the time to check. To what end, he wasn't sure.

Before the apartment house in which he had established his ineffectual hideout, he trotted to the closest Transport FS call box and summoned a hover cab. He made no effort to use the manual controls, they were slower than the automated robo guidance of the vehicle. He dialed the entertainment area of town that Paula Klein had taken him to several days before.

He wasn't going to be able to use Transport FS hover cars once the pursuit got under way. Security would be able to monitor every one in the cty, but for the present he felt still safe. He dismissed the car half a block from his destination and proceeded to the effective class speakeasy on foot.

He found even less difficulty in entering than he had expected. He simply stood before the tell-screen and a voice said, "You are recognized Techno Morris. You may enter."

He pushed through into the speakeasy rooms beyond and a few heads went up at his entrance. He forced himself to take it easy and drifted to a table where an animated discussion was taking place. He made himself listen for a few minutes, his facial expression registering interest, although he was tensed like a spring, inside.

Rex recognized one or two of the debaters from his former visit. One was the heavy-set junior effective who had been railing against motherhood the last time. Now he was saying, "It's an antiquated institution. It fitted the conditions that applied a thousand years ago, possibly even a couple of centuries ago but now it hangs on through sheer inertia."

From the side of his mouth, Rex said to the man standing next to him, "What're they discussing?"

"Marriage," the other said, and turned back to the debaters.

"This is how it sums up," the speaker said. "To quote an old jingle:

"Higamous hogamous, woman's monogamous

"Hogamous higamous, man is polygamous

"That's the way it is in nature. It's a man's instinct to impregnate as many females of the species as he can. Keeps the race going. It's a woman's to secure herself a protector and provider to take care of her and her infant during the period she is incapacitated. That keeps the race going too. Very good. In primitive clan society it was pretty well figured out. The community as a whole took care of all its members, and society was a matriarchy in which the women made the rules and regulations. However, with the coming of metal tools and weapons—which women weren't capable of using to the extent men were —and of privately owned property, the matriarchy gave way to the patriarchy, and women took a back seat. Man, now head of his own individual family, wanted to make sure the children he supported were his own, wanted to make sure his property descended to his sons. So what did he invent in the way of insurance? Virginity and adultery. In entering marriage, women were forced to have the one, to refrain from the other. And that's the basis of marriage as we know it still today."

"Well, what's wrong with it?" somebody demanded.

"It no longer applies," the plump speaker said reason-

139

ably. "Neither woman nor child depends on the father as a provider. Society takes care of both. Nor is the inheritance of property of a great deal of importance aside from family keepsakes and such. The institution of marriage is antiquated and so are such corollaries of it as a woman's virginity and prohibitions against adultery."

"So what do you propose as an alternative?" Rex Morris' neighbor asked skeptically.

"Complete promiscuity," the other told him, his voice indicating that nothing was more obvious. "Let two—or more, for that matter—people live together just so long as they're happy together. Then let them split, as soon as one, or both, are no longer happy."

"Fine," said somebody else, "but how do you keep any record of children at all? How do you know who belongs to who? Who your father is, who your relatives are?"

"Go back to the matriarchal system. Take your mother's name instead of your father's," the junior effective said reasonably. "It always has been said that it's a wise man who knows his father. But everybody knows his mother."

"Great Scott," Rex Morris muttered under his breath. He had stopped being of any interest at all to anyone in the room, so he sauntered on, trying to remember the route over which Paula Klein had taken him on the day of the raid.

It wasn't too big a problem, since one room led off the other and he finally found himself in the corridor which led to the small office and the senior effective known as Mike. He didn't bother to announce himself at the door but pushed his way through.

The florid faced effective looked up from the desk, scowled for a moment in lack of recognition. Then he said, "Rex Morris, Paula Klein's friend. How'd you make out the other day?"

Rex found a chair on the other side of the desk and sat down in it. "What interests me," he said coldly, "is how you made out. How you're back here in business again so soon."

Mike scowled again, in puzzlement over the tone of voice. "Oh, I got released after the usual routine."

"That's what I meant," Rex said. "What usual routine are you talking about?"

The other stared at him for a long moment. He said finally, "What did you want, Techno Morris?"

Rex Morris brought from his pocket the orange colored identity cum credit card he had taken from Matt Edgeworth. He held it up negligently knowing that at the distance involved neither name nor identity photo could be made out. "The name is Technician Morris," he said, "and although my appointment is in the western section of the Technate, my rank holds here. We don't put up with speakeasies where I'm from and this whole atmosphere disgusts me. I'm arresting you and taking you in. And this time, Mike, you won't be released after a *usual routine.*"

The other's expression of surprise had turned to one of contempt.

"Listen," he said, "why don't you do a little thinking before jumping into something you don't know anything about? I'm telling you, you wouldn't have me down at headquarters for ten minutes. Do you think a place like this could operate for a single day without connections, without protection?"

Rex Morris let his face register disbelief and then suspicion.

He said, "You're lying. What you're suggesting is that higher-ups are protecting this . . . this nonconformist, controversial hotbed."

Mike looked at him in open wonderment. "And you're the son of Leonard Morris, eh? The guy who got such a name for sounding off. How things can change." He leaned forward and his voice got harder. "Look here, Technician. Things might be different out west, but here in the capital we got protection. Plenty of it. You know who I'd go to if somebody with your rank gave me any guff?"

Rex said softly, "No, who?"

Mike told him.

Rex stared for a long, unbelieving moment. Then he said, "Then why the raid the other day? Where was your protection then?"

Mike spread his hands. "Atmosphere. Who'd want to come to a speakeasy if it wasn't forbidden, illegal, under the table? Makes it romantic, I suppose."

On the wall the tell-screen lit up and Matt Edgeworth's grim face looked out at them. Momentarily startled, Rex Morris at first thought it was a personal call, rather than a general city-wide broadcast.

Edgeworth bit out, "We of the Security FS have flushed one of the nihilists who have been committing acts of violence including assassination. This dangerous criminal is still at large, after fighting his way out of a trap. He is desperate and armed. All security ranks are ordered to fire first and upon sight. The nihilist mentality is such that he may attempt to take his own life, upon threat of capture by blowing himself up, with his captors. He is known to be in the possession of bombs. I repeat, fire first and on sight. All citizens belonging to other functional sequences, upon sighting this man, should immediately report him to the nearest Security officer. The following photos are of the criminal Rex Morris."

The screen began flashing moving shots of Rex, taken from different angles and from varying distances. Rex wondered briefly where Edgeworth had been able to dig them up so quickly.

Even as the photographs were showing, Matt Edgeworth's voice went on urgently. "Patriotic citizens are urged to stand firm against this menace. Indications are that high ranking names are involved in the nihilist conspiracy. No one's life or position is safe until the plot has been completely exposed and dealt with."

The fat was in the fire now. When the broadcast ended, Rex sighed and brought the gun from his pocket and trained it on Mike who was watching him nervously.

"Stand up," Rex commanded, coming to his own feet.

Mike stood, his hands raised. "Now look here . . ." he began.

"Quiet," Rex told him, "and possibly I won't have to kill you."

Mike paled. "Look, I gotta wife and . . ."

"I'll keep that in mind," Rex said. "Now turn your back."

"You're not gonna . . ."

"Turn around," Rex snapped. When the other did so, he clipped him with the butt of the gun on the back of the head. The senior effective collapsed forward to the floor.

Rex Morris turned his eyes up briefly in another short prayer—to whatever diety agnostics call upon in stress—this time that the man wasn't seriously hurt. He had no time to check.

He opened the door to the closet, fumbled around to find the door by which he and Paula Klein had escaped during the other day's raid. He pushed through it and into the narrow corridor beyond, retracing the route of a few days before. In a few minutes he was out on the street before the hotel.

He summoned a hover car as quickly as possible, knocked out its tell-screen with the butt of his gun, threw it onto manual control and made his way across the city.

He wasn't up on the abilities of the Security FS. He knew they had of recent years had little opportunity, little need to exercise, the ultra-measures they probably had at their command. It had been a long time since crime, political or otherwise, had been a major item. He was hoping the SFS was rusty. That the sort of dragnet that must be part of their arsenal would take time, the more the better, to put into operation. However, he was aghast at the speed with which Edgeworth had gotten on the air.

On top of the urgency under which he was operating, his mind was awhirl. He couldn't reconcile the developments of the past few hours with lifetime beliefs and experiences. He was in far over his head.

He pulled down a wide boulevard near the river, left the air cushion hover car and took to his feet. The broken tell-screen was going to be automatically reported to the Transport FS and possibly Security was already monitoring all cars. It behooved him to get out of the vicinity with as much speed as he could manage without attracting attention.

He reasoned that at this stage, comparatively few pedestrians would have seen the broadcast that Matt Edgeworth had made. He had no doubt that after it had been repeated a few times, a few score times, over the next few hours that everyone in the city would be a potential danger to him, but not quite yet.

He found the apartment house he wanted and took the appropriate elevator to the top floor. At the door of Lizzy Mihm's residence he pushed the little black button as he had seen his uncle do the day of the cocktail party. He realized glumly that this was one of the few places in town he dare visit. Had he announced himself in the ordinary manner, and had Lizzy Mihm seen that broadcast, as she almost surely had . . .

The door opened and the hefty, short statured Lizzy was beaming at him. "Why . . . *Rex*. William's dear, *dear* nephew from the west."

As the door opened, Rex Morris had slid his right foot forward to block its closing, but on the face of things, Lizzy Mihm hadn't seen Matt Edgeworth's broadcast. He wondered why. The Security Technician had been able to utilize the emergency facilities to go on every tell-screen in the area, whether or not it was turned on, and whether or not it had been in use at the time for some other purpose. However, there was no point in questioning good fortune.

"*Do* come in," Lizzy was saying. She had a beefy, several ringed hand on his sleeve as she led him into one of her living rooms. She giggled archly. "I don't believe I had the chance to tell you before that your father used to be one of my *best* beaux back before I met Freddy."

"Freddy?" Rex said blankly.

"My husband. I'm afraid your father was much too . . . well, *disputatious* for little me. *Gracious*, the terrible reputation he did bring on himself."

They were in the living room. Lizzy Mihm bustied about like a chickless biddy hen, insisting on getting a pil-

144

low to stuff behind him in the already overstuffed chair. She bustled some more at the autobar, brought him a long drink of unknown ingredients.

Finally she wound up across from him, her face beaming. "Now, what is it, Rex?—now you must call me Elizabeth. A young man doesn't call on a, well, practically middle-aged woman like me unless he has something *important* in mind. Now does he?"

Silently he thanked her for allowing him to get to the point without unseeming haste.

"Techna Mihm . . ."

"Elizabeth, now!"

"Well, yes . . . Elizabeth. Uncle Bill said something the other day that just came to mind a little while ago. He said that on occasion you've entertained the Supreme Technician here."

"*Jack?* Why of course, my dear, *dear* boy. Jack was . . ." she giggled here . . ." why Jack was one of my boyfriends. Before I met Freddy, of course." She put a finger to her lips and thought a moment. "Jack was just before I met your lovely, *lovely* father."

Rex winced. He had never heard his father so misaptly described.

He said, "Uh . . . Elizabeth, it's very important for me to talk to the Supreme Technician."

She blinked at him. "Oh, dear. It is?" She looked at her watch. "Well, you mean today?"

"Just as soon as possible." He made his voice very earnest, not that it took much of an effort.

She put a hefty hand to her mouth and went, "Tch, tch, tch."

He said urgently, "This is very important, Elizabeth."

"Of course, my dear, dear boy, I believe you. You look quite like your father in his most *urgent* mood. Let me see, I suppose there's just nothing for it. We'll have to break in on his dinner. He'll never be in his office this time of day."

He stared at her. "You mean you know John Mc-Farlane well enough to intrude . . . uh, that is, visit him, well, just any time?" He had been thinking only in terms of a tell-screen conversation, at the very best.

She fluttered at him. "Rex, do let me tell you a secret. Men with ranks such as Jack's aren't nearly as busy as everyone supposes. I know that you'll think this is just *awful* of me, and controversial, but these days such offices are mostly, well, figurehead positions. And sometimes I suspect that's been true—now you'll think this just awful of me—practically all through history. When a position gets so big that one man simply can't handle it —why then one man simply stops handling it. No matter if his job is king, president or supreme technician."

He didn't know if he quite followed that or not. He said, "Well, then . . ."

"Wait just a moment until I get into something, well, more *flattering*. You see Rexie . . ."

Rex Morris inwardly flinched again.

". . . Jack is *still* one of my dearest boy friends. Now that Freddy has passed away of course." She swept from the room, giggling archly over her shoulder.

"Great Scott," Rex muttered softly.

Lizzy Mihm was evidently one of the few persons still in town who bothered to have a privately owned limousine. She flutteringly explained as they stepped into it in the servo-term in the basement of her building that she was just too nervous to go about the trouble of dialing a Transport FS garage and having one sent when she wished to go somewhere.

"I'm always in *such* a hurry," she twittered.

Rex murmured something and climbed in beside her. It was a lucky break for him. At least this vehicle wouldn't be monitored. Surely there weren't many cars of this antiquity still in existence. He suspected it was an old electro model, although he had never seen one before. Trust Lizzy Mihm to have an antique like this.

She dialed the White House and settled back to her gushing chatter while the car merged into the traffic. She must have had private coordinates, Rex decided, when the vehicle went through the guarded entry gates without pause. Four uniformed sentries snapped to the salute at the ancient vehicle's approach.

Lizzy Mihm giggled. "They all know my car," she said happily. "Now that's one value of having your own, all your *very* own."

Rex had mental fingers crossed. This was all going unbelievably well. Impossibly, unbelievably well. After a day of repeated blows which had crumpled plans years in the making, this was coming much too easily.

They buzzed past the front portico, so famed in newscasts, and proceeded to the rear of the building. Lizzy bustled from the car, explaining some of the workings of the White House as she went, and hardly waiting for Rex.

"It's all such a bother, you know," she said. "Poor Jack. He'd just love to spend his time, all of his time, I suspect, fishing off Yucatan or in Canada. But all this *bother*. He has to shake somebody's hand, or give somebody an award. Or have a Tri-Di of him greeting some committee. You'll never believe me, but he puts in a full four hour day, four days a week, like anybody else."

Which seemed to negate her earlier claim that John McFarlane was only a figurehead, Rex decided.

She swept up the stairs of the rear entrance, fluttered a cheerful welcome to the armed Security engineer there and hustled into the interior. The SFS man evidently didn't particularly notice Rex. Lizzy Mihm was as at home as she had earlier implied and evidently anyone with her was automatically in.

Chattering, she led him down a short hallway to a door, once again guarded, this time by two Security officers of engineer rank. Lizzy beamed at them, said, "Hello, Morton. And how are you Ernest? Is your dear, *dear* wife any better?"

Ernest mumbled something in return as he opened the door for her.

Lizzy Mihm swept on through, Rex trailing behind.

He had expected the personal apartments of the Supreme Technician, John McFarlane. Instead, he was in a moderately large conference room.

Confronting him, most of them seated about a heavy mahogany table, were possibly thirty-five or forty men and women. Of them, Rex had met three or four personally either through his father or uncle. Most of the others he recognized from news casts, publicity shots, articles in popular publications. There was a hush as the newcomers entered.

Lizzy Mihm said incisively, "May I introduce Rex Morris our currently most notorious citizen of the Technate?"

A tall, thin man who had been standing to one side, glass in hand at an autobar, was the first to raise his voice above the resulting hum of conversation. It was John McFarlane, Supreme Technician of the Technate of North America.

He raised his glass in a half salute to Rex Morris. "We were wondering how to get hold of you," he said. "Welcome to the ultimate speakeasy."

19.

"Speakeasy?" Rex Morris said. His eyes went around the room uncomprehendingly.

From half way down the table Warren Klein, dressed in his gray uniform of Prime Technician of the Security FS, said dryly, "And even here, you see, we have police. Thanks for missing me the other night, Morris, but next time, please, don't make it quite so close."

Rex Morris' eyes went from the Security chief to the Supreme Technician and then to Lizzy Mihm. Somehow she looked different, her fluttery aspects a thing of the past.

Supreme Technician McFarlane took mercy on him.

"Sit down, Rex," he said. "We've gathered for the purpose of meeting you after receiving a call from Elizabeth that you were on the way. We'll have individual introductions later. Now let it suffice for me to say that with one or two exceptions, unavoidable absentations, we have present the Congress of Prime Technicians and a dozen or more retired holders of the same rank. Plus. . . ." and he bowed his head here to Elizabeth Mihm ". . . various other honored members of this—speakeasy."

An easy, unhurried stranger in the garb of a Prime Technician brought Rex a drink from the autobar, ushered him to one of the table's empty chairs.

The room had fallen silent now. Most of its occupants

were staring at the newcomer with open but friendly curiosity. Most of them drifted to the conference table and took seats.

The Supreme Technician took his place at the table's head. He said, "First of all, let us thank you for your efforts."

"My efforts?" Rex Morris repeated inanely.

"Yes. You see, they were directed toward a most worthy end and one which we pursue ourselves." He cleared his throat. "Although your methods were somewhat more enthusiastic, let us say."

Rex Morris caught hold of himself enough to blurt indignantly, "My efforts were ultimately aimed at ending the Technate!"

"Ummm," John McFarlane nodded, "so are ours."

Rex Morris stared at him. Absolutely nothing made sense.

"Let's have some background," an overweight, elderly man clad in robes said from across the table. With a shock Rex Morris realized it was the Supreme Bishop of the Temple.

"Yes, obviously," McFarlane nodded. He turned to Rex again. "I don't know to what extent you've studied the history of revolution down through the ages. Even a comparatively brief examination of the subject reveals that the modern revolutionary finds himself in a unique position. You do consider yourself a revolutionary, of course?"

"I suppose so," Rex said defiantly. He kept his eyes on the older man's face.

"In the past," the Supreme Technician went on, "revolutions were accomplished by dissatisfied, enraged masses, contrary to some popular belief that would put them at the door of small groups of malcontents." He pursed his lips. "There are any number of examples. Jefferson, Madison, Franklin, Washington and the other so-called Revolutionary Forefathers, found themselves hard put to run fast enough to stay out in front of the revolting colonists. Robespierre, Danton and Marat were pushed by the mob into their feudalistic destroying stands. More recent is the

Russian example. Lenin and Zinoviev were in Switzerland when the Soviets began to form. Trotsky was in New York and Stalin, a third stringer at that time, was in exile in Siberia. They had to move fast to get back to Petrograd and take over the reins thrown to them."

He shrugged. "I suppose the point is made. To get to our own times, we find a unique situation. *There is no downtrodden mass of dissatisfied slaves, serfs or proletarians.* A fundamental change in our society is needed, is demanded by historical necessity but the overwhelming majority of our population are at present content with institutions as they are."

"This doesn't make sense," Rex Morris said bitterly. "If you, yourselves, are opposed to this form of government, why not resign? Under the Technate our culture is stagnating like never before in modern history."

McFarlane nodded. "Correct. But resign to what end? Would our resignations abolish the Technate? Obviously not. There are a thousand, a million, others willing to step into our positions." He twisted his mouth wryly. "Matt Edgeworth is an example."

Rex Morris sank back into his chair. He wished he had more time for thought. He was being pushed confusingly fast.

"There's another element here," McFarlane said thoughtfully, "that possibly you've never considered. When fundamental changes begin to take place in a social system, those who inaugurate them are not always spared the ultimate results. Using the Russian example again, we have the elements who originally precipitated the revolt against the Czar. I am speaking of Kerensky who represented the liberal Social Democrats who wished to abolish feudalism and establish a government based on Western lines. But the revolution got out of hand, once it began to move, and Kerensky found himself a fugitive and his government as much in the discard as was that of the Czar."

"I don't get your point," Rex said, although he was beginning to.

McFarlane said dryly, "Once in control of a governmental system, it is not always easy to relinquish it safely,

151

even though you so desire. While we of the Congress of Prime Technicians subscribe to the belief that the Technate must go, we are not anxious to sacrifice ourselves, physically, in the going. Your own pseudo-nihilistic measures were actually not meant to do more than startle our people into movement—the next revolutionist who comes along might be of more ambitious designs."

Rex thought about that.

The Prime Technician of the Entertainment FS, seated at the other end of the long table, said, "And before it was all over, you yourself, Rex Morris, and possibly the members of your family, might find themselves lined up against a handy wall."

And Rex thought about that for a moment.

He blurted suddenly, "Why, all these years, have you persecuted my father? From what you're saying, you feel much the same way he does."

"Exactly the same," the Supreme Bishop said agreeably.

John McFarlane sid, "Who in the whole land was better suited than Leonard Morris to defy our conventions, sneer at our fear of controversial subjects, our conforming, our horror at the very idea of any changes in the status quo? As our sole surviving Hero of the Technate he is as near untouchable as anyone. Leonard was the spark that enabled a thousand speakeasies to open their doors, who set a million nonconforming tongues to wagging. It's at least a step."

The door by which Rex Morris and Elizabeth Mihm had entered fifteen minutes earlier, opened behind them. Rex's eyes went to it, and then widened.

"Hello, son," the newcomer said.

"Dad!"

The old boy grinned at him. "I wish you'd discussed your project with me a bit before you took off, boy. On a hurry up call, I just came in from Taos on the rocket."

Rex Morris was on his feet. "I . . . I thought you had suffered enough. I wanted any possible consequences to be on me alone."

His father chuckled. "Well, at least we know where

152

you stand. I've never been really sure, which is the prime reason I never told you about the existence of this . . . . speakeasy, club . . . ." He chuckled again and looked around at the room's occupants. "Or what would you call it, an underground cell?"

Everyone laughed. Leonard Morris had the ability to lighten the mood. The Prime Technician who had been seated next to Rex relinquished his chair to the noted scientist and found another.

John McFarlane came around the table to shake hands, exchange a dozen words with the older Morris, and then resumed his place.

"Let us proceed," he said. "To sum up, our impetuous young friend Rex Morris is of the opinion that under the Technate man stagnates. We agree. Friend Rex on his own initiative, arrived at the conclusion that sparks must be struck to bring the average citizen, Techno, Engineer or Effective, out of his mental rut and be made to realize that the present hierarchical governmental form must not be permanent. We agree. Thus far, we have been somewhat hesitant in our efforts. We have tolerated, indeed, have secretly encouraged, the speakeasy where anyone can be as controversial as he wishes and where the most extreme ideas can be advanced. We have encouraged the growth of the so-called gossip news commentators, who in the name of humor and entertainment snipe at our institutions. Obviously, however, this is not enough. We must increase our efforts and attract new and aggressive blood." He looked about the table. "Perhaps a motion is in order."

Prime Technician Warren Klein came to his feet. "I make a motion that upon my resignation, Techno Rex Morris be appointed Prime Technician of the Security Functional Sequence." A wan smile touched his pale lips. "And while I am standing, I might as well tender my resignation, something I have looked forward to for years, due to both age and health."

Rex Morris was on his feet again. "Great Scott!" he blurted.

Elizabeth Mihm was looking at him amusedly. Even in

153

all the turmoil of his thoughts, he found time to wonder how he could ever have thought her less than cool, efficient and hard headed. She said, "But Rex, dear boy, you came to our city, didn't you, looking for an appointment. You've reached the age when you must do your share of the Technate's work. You have ten years of your life to devote to society."

He glared at her. "Prime Technician! Why, I don't know *anything* about the Security Functional Sequence." He cast his eyes wildly around the table. "Are you all mad?"

John McFarlane said seriously, "We have effectives and we have engineers who can handle details most efficiently. What we need, Rex Morris, is a man of principle and ideals to sit with us here at the highest level—and plan the ending of our socio-economic system, to be replaced with something better. You fill the qualifications. The other obligations of your office can be learned."

"And I'd be over all such Security officials as, well, Matt Edgeworth?"

Warren Klein said slowly, "Don't underestimate the value of our Matt Edgeworths. At least such men have ambition, drive, courage and—dreams. It is possibly of such types that the new society will be formed."

"What new society?" Rex said desperately. "You're throwing these punches faster than I can assimilate them. What do you have in mind for the future? What will the new government look like?"

His father looked at him strangely. "We're the ruling class, son. Radical changes, peaceful or otherwise, don't come about from the top down. No matter how weary those on top might be. They come from the bottom up."

"You mean you don't know?"

The Supreme Bishop said gently, "Within our own group here, we have a half dozen theories. Undoubtedly, within the speakeasies and wherever else men exchange ideas, new ones will be proposed. It remains to be seen what our people as a whole will ultimately turn to."

Rex Morris sat back in his chair still once again. He said, as though talking to himself, "I came here to confront the Supreme Technician. To tell him that the government was corrupt. To warn him of Matt Edgeworth. To warn him that Warren Klein himself was tolerating and protecting the speakeasies. To throw up to him that the Technate was rotten from within and demand that changes be made. That and similar things I came to shout at him. And what do I wind up with . . . ?"

John McFarlane said to his assembled Congress of Prime Technicians, "If there are no objections, the motion of Warren Klein will be passed and Rex Morris be appointed Prime Technician of Security."

The meeting broke up into smaller groups, who took their turns in shaking hands with their new member of Congress. Each spoke a few words. Each offered their congratulations.

His mind still awhirl, as quickly as he could Rex got Warren Klein aside. The former security head, seeing the younger man's confusion, chuckled and said, "Don't worry about it. I'll stick around for awhile showing you the ropes. You'll have little trouble.,'

Rex said, "You know, there's one thing that has a top priority. I'm going to have to seek out your sister, Paula, and make amends for my conduct with her. It was, of course, protective covering. I was trying to put over the idea that I was the most conforming of all young men that ever conformed."

Warren Klein grinned his amusement. "I don't believe you'll have too very much trouble. In spite of surface reactions, I've somehow got the impression that my impetuous Paula looks on you with a kindly eye."

Rex said, "All right. Fine. But there's something even more immediate. There's a call out by Matt Edgeworth for any Security FS man to shoot me on sight."

Klein pursed his lips and nodded. "That's right, I'd forgotten, for the moment. I didn't catch the thing myself. I'll get on the phone and put things right."

Rex said worriedly, "He put it on every screen in this part of the country and worded it in such a way that anyone with a gun would start firing immediately. And another thing. You can't get any more ambitious than Edgeworth and he's not going to take kindly to my being put above him, particularly in view of the fact that he sounded off with some of his opportunistic ambitions to me."

"I see. Hmmm, yes, Matt was always on the impetuous side." Warren Klein hesitated, then called to the Supreme Technician who was standing nearby talking to Elizabeth Mihm, in light tones. "John, could we speak to you?"

John McFarlane excused himself and came over.

Warren Klein explained the situation and McFarlane nodded and said easily, "No problem. We'll go over to the Security FS building and you, Warren, can introduce me on a Technate-wide broadcast. I'll say a few words, announce that a great mistake has been made. We'll lay the onus on the shoulders of our ambitious Technician, remove him from his position, and bring the whole matter to a quick close."

"Obviously, the thing to do," Warren Klein agreed. "I'll order up your car, sir."

They retraced the route by which Elizabeth Mihm had brought Rex to the White House hardly more than an hour before, stepping into John McFarlane's chauffeur driven limousine at the back door and then driving around to the front portico and hence to the street. The three of them sat in the back and to Rex's jumbled mind the conversation seemed idiotically light in view of the great moment of the situation. Life simply was not moving fast enough for him. He was burning with eagerness to get this confounded matter over with and to get into really deep, significant conversations with everybody from his father to the Supreme Bishop of the Temple.

They whipped out the entry gates and headed for the skyscraper which housed the Security FS.

The car slammed to a sudden halt and for a few whirl-wind split moments life became for Rex Morris brief snatches of impressions . . . . Matt Edgeworth with some strange, large-calibered weapon cuddled in his arms, standing spread-legged in the street . . . . a squad of Security Junior Engineers and Senior Engineers behind him, all heavily armed, all large, brutal looking types

156

. . . . the chauffeur jumping from the car and snatching for a holstered hand weapon, and then crumbling, cut almost in half . . . . something black being thrown toward the car, even as Rex and Warren Klein tried to climb out through the door on the far side from Edgeworth and his men, but being handicapped by the bloody, inert body of the Supreme Technician . . .

And then a great, searing world of yellow and orange flame and a unique, unbearable, all encompassing pain . . .

And then it was all over and it could be left to others to accomplish a revolution, peaceful or otherwise, against the Technate of North America. Rex Morris no longer cared.

www.ingramcontent.com/pod-product-compliance
Lightning Source LLC
Chambersburg PA
CBHW020648180626
46816CB00003B/1179